The D
Beue

R. E. GUTHRIE

ISBN-10: 1717589243
ISBN-13: 9781717589248

THANKS

With special thanks to Steve, Chris, Rachael and Linda whose support and encouragement made this book happen.

PREFACE

The author would like to state that it is a criminal offence to trespass on the railway. Trespassing on the railway is a serious issue which can lead to fatal consequences.

CONTENTS

ACKNOWLEDGMENTS

With thanks to Torp Illustrations for help with the front cover.

"No man is an island" John Donne

CHAPTER 1 - ARRIVAL

It was strange that the gate was open. On my three previous visits to the house I had always been unable to open it.

I peered through and slowly stepped down the roughly made stone stairway until I stood beside the railway tracks. I looked in both directions and could see the lines stretching away. To my left they climbed a slight incline until they reached the horizon. To my right they ran straight for about two hundred yards until they disappeared around the corner.

I sighed deeply and contentedly. The spring sunshine was warm on my face and I felt decidedly happy. The world was calm but not silent. Somewhere in the distance a tractor droned in nearby fields, and by my feet, blackbirds stirred up last autumn's leaves looking for grubs to eat. Magpies cawed and insects buzzed. But there were no trains. Not yet.

I slowly returned up the steps through the gate

and pushed it shut. It swung quite easily, until it was almost closed, at which point it needed a slight shove to get it into place. The latch clicked confidently and so I tried to see if it would open again. It did. Nothing to mend there then. First problem solved.

It is always exciting, that first day in a new house. I had moved in the afternoon before, just as it was getting dark and had merely spent the evening cleaning, dusting and exploring where to put all my stuff as I began to make a start on the boxes that needed to be emptied. There was no rush and no hurry and I delighted myself putting things first here and then there to see where they belonged the best. I took plenty of breaks for cups of tea (the kettle had, of course, been unpacked first), before arranging some cushions on the floor, dressing the duvet in a clean cover, the pillows likewise and collapsing into an exhausted sleep.

A new house and a new start.

That first day the list of jobs was joyously endless. More cleaning, more unpacking and more exploring my new home: what worked and what didn't? I had a feeling that lots of things would not work, the place was so ramshackle and run down. I excitedly felt that I was going to manage somehow, and looked forward to solving all these problems one by one. This was after all my dream house, and at the moment I felt nothing could spoil it. My fridge and kettle seemed to work, so at least some of the plug sockets were ok, but the cooker was doing nothing. Luckily an old camping ring would do for heating anything a microwave couldn't handle. The gate at the bottom of the garden was a bonus. Now I would not have to try to unjam that, even though it only led to the railway.

I had fallen in love with the place from the first moment I saw it. An old railway cottage that used to belong to the crossing keeper in the days when the road actually crossed the railway. Nowadays the lane had long since been abandoned so it merely led to the house and no further. As the railways became less labour intensive, the house ceased to be a crossing keeper's home and for many years was just used as a storage facility by Network Rail or its predecessors. It was shabby and unloved, meaning that when it was put on the market for sale as a home only the bravest of fools would buy the place, which was why I had picked up a bargain. The estate agent had clearly been bemused, yet relieved, to get the place off his hands. He was metaphorically rubbing them throughout our conversations and unlike most house buying experiences this one went through with unconventional speed. I had always longed to live deep in the countryside, miles from everywhere. My old life of people, bustle and stress was now behind me. Harbouring a passion for trains for as long as I could remember, finding this house, next to a quiet railway line, was the culmination of several dreams. I had made a ridiculous offer after my second viewing and was surprised when it was so quickly accepted.

More cleaning to do and a bedroom to decorate, so after a second brew it was time to explore upstairs properly. I already knew which of the two upstairs rooms would be my bedroom. The larger of the two faced the front, but was also dark and dreary, looking north. The back bedroom seemed to be a sun trap, more welcoming and more cosy. Most importantly, it overlooked the garden, the gate and the railway. As I looked out of the window, rabbits were nibbling the grasses on the far side of the line and two crows suddenly launched themselves into the air from a tree to the right of the gate. Strangely, the gate was open again and yet I was sure I had shut it after my experiment earlier. Perhaps the wind had caught it and the latch was not as firm as it had appeared; although today there was barely a breeze.

Scrubbing the floors was going to be a pain with just a kettle to heat the water. The new boiler was not being fitted until Monday. Today was Saturday, so it was up and down stairs with a bowl and a brush to scrub those floorboards. Gratifyingly it didn't take as long as I thought it would, and cleaning away twenty years of dust and grime revealed a passable sturdy floor that even seemed to have some of its old stain and polish on it. Perhaps all the dirt had actually provided some sort of protection. Tomorrow, after painting the walls, I'd put the blue rug down and move the bedroom furniture in.

CHAPTER 2

Next morning I was up early, painting the four walls of the back bedroom. I'd bought a few tins of paint before the move, knowing there would be nowhere nearby to buy any once I arrived. I chose pale blue for the walls, since the bright sunshine kept the room light enough. White paint would do for the bedroom at the front of the house. With a cheerful playlist on the iPod and no interruptions, I made good progress and had all four walls done adequately by just after one o'clock. I probably made a strange sight singing away to myself half covered in paint and dressed in my oldest clothes, but there was no one to see me. It wasn't a professional job, in fact it was a bit slapdash - my excuse being that perfection is the privilege of the gods.

Sunday lunch was a very simple meal. A large bowl of nuts, seeds and raisins and plenty of tea. I finished off the last of the loaf that I had brought with me but it was getting pretty stale and I left most of it for the birds on the tiny bit of lawn spared by the encroaching undergrowth. I'd be able to stock up with more food tomorrow when I ventured into Newstead, the local town. I sat and ate outside having brought a small fold up chair into the garden. It was warm and sunny out of the breeze. The overgrown garden was offering me protection from the elements. The gate, I was pleased to notice, was firmly shut ever since I had come down yesterday, before dark, to shut it again. Once more I had ventured down those few steps onto the railway track. Again the tracks had been silent and I hadn't heard a single train since the late passenger service had rattled past, just before midnight, the first evening I'd moved in. I knew that there must have been some trains on the line at weekends even if there were not as many as during the week. Maybe the line was closed for engineering work. This was confirmed when, finishing lunch I had meandered through the gate and down onto the tracks. Gazing up the line, to my left, I became aware of the sound of boots crunching along the ballast behind me. I turned to see two men wearing hi-viz jackets coming down the track. To dart back up the steps and through the gate now would have looked odd, so I thought the best policy was to remain where I was, as they'd probably already seen me. They looked up as they approached and I nodded.

"Afternoon," I said. They nodded in acknowledgement and stopped walking.

"You live in there do you?" the one on the right asked. I agreed with another quick nod and a smile. "Good sturdy old house that is. They built them to last in them days. Trains'll wake you up in the morning, mind."

"I haven't heard many yet," I replied.

"None till tomorrow. Closed the line. Fixing that tunnel back there. Lining keeps coming loose and drivers are always reporting bricks on the track. Beggar of a job. We used to use your place to store equipment, you know. Never could get that gate there open. Always had to walk round the side to the front. Right nuisance it was lugging everything round there. How d'you manage to get it open then?"

Not knowing how to answer, I merely said, "Oh I just had to loosen and oil the hinges."

"Shame we couldn't have done that," came the reply. "Not much use to us now. Nor you neither only leading down here."

He said goodbye and the two continued walking on their way. I watched after them, and the one who hadn't spoken glanced back towards me, giving me what I can only describe as a perplexed look. I watched them trudge onwards up the incline towards wherever they were heading.

I turned back up the steps to retreat indoors. As I crossed the garden the sun went in and I felt a chill wind on my back. The gate rattled impertinently. I returned upstairs and continued painting the skirting board in the back bedroom. It was soon done and I stood up to stretch my back and wonder whether the smell of paint would diminish enough for me to sleep in here tonight, getting fed up with cushions on the floor downstairs already. I was keen to start living in my new home properly.

The cottage was built along with the railway line in the 1880s. I presume that it housed various crossing keepers and their families, although with only two bedrooms, life would have been rather cramped with more than a couple of children. Belying its unkempt appearance, the survey on the house had revealed it to be of sound construction, with no evidence of any damp, despite its age. Covered in a kind of milky, pink pebbledash, that might even be deciding it was time to turn grey, it did not have an unpleasant appearance, especially when viewed from the lane. The house was approached by turning a slight corner, and the enshrouding hedgerows virtually concealed it from more than a hundred yards away. The place was even connected to the gas mains. However, inside the heating had obviously been provided by traditional coal fires, long since unused. These I hoped to resurrect before the onset of winter. The simple kitchen boiler I had opted for would merely heat the water and five small radiators all to be fitted in the easiest to reach places. "A unique property, Sir," I remember the agent saying. I couldn't agree more.

There is no garden to the front. Simply a small patch of dusty gravel, enough room to park a car, and for another to turn round should one stray down the lane by accident, although this has not happened yet. The entrance to the lane about half a mile away (maybe it's less than that - unfamiliar roads always seem longer than they are) is blessed with no less than two *No Through Road* signs. There you will also find an isolated Royal Mail post box, which promises a collection six days a week, but does not state at what time. I can't help wondering that the lane, which had presumably once been a public right of way across the railway tracks, was no longer at least a footpath beyond the line, where the original lane had once gone. However, a study of the Ordnance survey map revealed no such path crossing here now. The old lane itself had actually only ever led to some disused farm buildings further across the fields. These did not exist any more to my knowledge, but I looked forward to exploring any remains. The arable farmland around the property was criss-crossed with massive hedgerows that yearned to overspill into tiny pockets of woodland. No doubt they provided habitat and shelter for a variety of woodland creatures: badgers, mice, rabbits I hoped. My previous life in the city had never offered such simple delights. I was ever optimistic.

I had a television, but the house had no aerial, and certainly nothing so obscene as a satellite dish. Fortunately I had no desire to watch it. As I prepared a simple but satisfying supper, the radio provided me with a quick yet uninspiring update on the news. My new surroundings were making me feel beautifully cut off from the outside world and I was devoid of any desire to rejoin it. That Sunday evening, I sat on my old armchair, feet up, listening to the sounds of the countryside stirring outside. Wearing a couple of sweaters kept me from feeling the chill. A small side-lamp placed on a wooden coffee table, and my old illuminated globe both cast a mellow light and I thought about how in the winter I should get the old fireplace working and be all snug. Before turning in, I stopped to gaze at the moonlight out of the front window; always a delight to someone who has lived so long in an urban environment polluted by street lamps and the constant strobing of passing car headlights. The cloudless sky was the deepest indigo and the silver stars vibrated as if they were eyes from the past. The bushes and trees rustled musically in the breeze. Somewhere an owl hooted. I wondered what time I would hear the first train tomorrow. As I undressed for bed, the one annoyance was that I couldn't find my keys.

CHAPTER 3

There was no need for the alarm clock that I had set for 6am in anticipation of the boiler fitter arriving at seven. I was up and about at least twenty minutes beforehand, possibly because that had been when the first train had rattled through. The mystery of the missing keys was soon solved during my constitutional wander outside with a morning brew. There at the end of the garden, just outside the open gate (I was sure I had shut it: it must have blown open again during the night, although I must have slept soundly for I never heard it) was my bunch of keys. I had no idea how I could have dropped them here without hearing them clatter to the ground, but my mind was distracted by the sight of the most amazing sunrise. The glowing red orb rising in the sky seemed to be like a large caricature of itself. As I stood and watched it slowly rise, it seemed to shrink and brighten back to its normal self but left me with an uplifted feeling and an eagerness to get on with the day.

I set about arranging tea and coffee for the workman, and then located all my bits and pieces for the trip into Newstead. This included unearthing my swimming trunks, since a weekend without a bath or shower had left me feeling distinctly grubby, never mind the spatters of paint that I had neglected on my arms. Ray the plumber arrived just after seven and said the boiler fitting would take him until about two o'clock that afternoon. He didn't need me about, and conscious that I would be in his way, I didn't stay for long. Leaving him my mobile phone number "just in case," I grabbed the car keys and set off to drive the six miles into town.

My parents would have approved of the morning swim, always concerned that I was keeping fit and healthy. I made a mental note to ring them again this evening with an update on how I was settling in. They worried about my chucking in the towel, giving up a good job, selling my nice, but boring, suburban property on the outskirts of the city, and "downsizing" to a hovel in the country.

After doing thirty lengths of the pool with the other early risers I made my way to the local supermarket. I stocked up with all the things I needed, and probably many that I didn't, plus enough tinned food to get me through the days when I couldn't be bothered to drive into town (I have no freezer, and can't think where I would have room to put one). The supermarket also stocked a minimal number of D.I.Y bits and pieces, but unfortunately no more tins of paint.

Leaving the car in the car park I decided on a quick walk into the town centre to remind myself of what was on offer. There was a stationery shop, a bakery, a traditional butcher's, a couple of chemists and luckily a cut-price, stock-it-high and sell-it-cheap general store, with a limited supply of paint, the brand of which I had never even heard of. I bought what I could carry, including another cheap set of five paintbrushes of varying sizes, and headed back to the car. By now the sunshine was invigorating and there was almost a feel of summer in the air. The residents were beginning to go about their business wearing sunglasses and rolling up their shirt sleeves. The cafe owners were busy arranging chairs and tables outside, in any available space, trying their utmost to scoop in more customers than each other. As I drove out of the town, I passed the station, so I pulled over to pick up a timetable, before heading back home.

Ray was busy banging something into place as I arrived. He grunted a response to my greeting and I set about stocking up the kitchen cupboards with my groceries. Wanting to avoid getting under his feet I thought I'd inspect the back bedroom and decide whether the smell of paint had faded enough for me to start moving the bedroom furniture in. I'd used the opportunity of the nice sunny morning, to leave the windows wide open. The house was isolated enough for intruders to be a rarity, and besides, Ray was around, his van parked out the front. I decided that the room was indeed fit for habitation but as I glanced down at the floor I noticed a large stone. Also, drawn on the floor boards, again towards the middle of the room, was a chalked cross, about the size of a human hand. I then realised that Ray must have been up here doing something towards fitting the radiators tomorrow. I picked up the stone, which on closer examination seemed more like a piece of brick, placed it on the mantelpiece and went to get the blue rug to try it out on the floor. Reminded of the fact that the room ought not be furnished during the fitting of the pipes and radiators I resigned myself to another night on the lounge floor with the cushions. Nevertheless, as I laid it out, the rug certainly looked as if it was going to be an ideal covering for the floor, leaving a decent perimeter of floorboards visible all around the room. I rolled it up again, and went downstairs to see how Ray was doing.

Within an hour, Ray finished up and checked that everything was in order. He packed his things and wondered aloud if his tape measure was in the van. I now had hot tap water, but would have to wait until tomorrow for the radiators and heating. Luckily the weather was being kind. For the rest of the day I kept myself busy emptying yet more boxes and wondering where the local tip was. My mountain bike would have to rest under some polythene until I could get some sort of garden shed. I ended the afternoon sitting in a patch of sunshine at the top of the steps by the back gate. The golden sunlight kissed my face, and the sky had faded to an exceptionally pale blue. Some spindly roses fought for space with a forsythia and an unruly lilac tree. I scanned the garden wondering how brutal to be when I started to cut it all back. This would have to be done if I was to have a chance of doing anything more than just sitting out here. Where, for example, could I hang out my washing? I glanced at my watch as the tell-tale rumble of an approaching train reached my ears. Ten past five. The train ran past, a blur of blue and black, heading out towards the coast. At the bottom of the steps my eyes fell upon a red tape measure. I couldn't understand why Ray would have brought it out here, and a few more questions began to stir somewhere in the back of my mind.

CHAPTER 4

I awoke the next day feeling cold and a quick glance out of the window revealed that the warm April mornings had beaten a retreat. Today was dull and a stiff breeze seemed to stir all the surrounding trees into an impatient mood. I had slept longer than I intended, and had just enough time to quickly wash and dress before I heard Ray's van slowly turn into the patch of gravel outside.

"Not such a nice day today," Ray said, stating the obvious as he set down his tool box.

I murmured in agreement and then said, "Oh I think I found your tape measure."

"Where did you find that then?"

"Under this tea-cloth on top of the fridge," I replied wondering why I was lying. He seemed satisfied and I took myself outside for a brew. This prompted me that I had forgotten to buy any teabags whilst in town yesterday. Frowning over this, helped me to decide what to do. I wanted to be out of the house whilst Ray worked, so a good walk exploring the local area seemed in order. Bored with unpacking and cleaning, a blustery stroll would clear my mind and might lead me to the village where I hoped to replenish my dwindling tea supply. The Ordnance Survey map showed a walk to the nearby village via the lane and then down the Newstead Road, although in the opposite direction to that which I had driven yesterday. A more direct pathway across the fields from the village station would bring me back to the Newstead Road close to where it met the lane to the house, providing a circular walk. I put on a fleece and a scarf and a woolly hat, leaving Ray to clatter about with the new pipes and radiators.

The local village had the slightly amusing name of Poppington, and the map seemed to show it as one of those sprawling villages of scattered groups of houses with no real centre. However, with a church, a pub and a railway station I certainly hoped there'd be a small convenience store somewhere. Perhaps I half remembered that the estate agent had mentioned a shop? If not I'd have to drive into Newstead again later. As I walked, a few things began to push themselves towards the front of my mind. Why had I been reluctant to tell Ray that his tape measure had been on the steps beside the railway? It obviously had something to do with the fact that my keys had also mysteriously appeared there too. The gate opening by itself could be part of the puzzle, but was easily explained by its age or even just the weather.

The walk to Poppington was about two miles and took around forty minutes. First I reached a T junction, next to a pub, imaginatively named *The*

Railway. This road merely took you down to the railway station, which I knew from the timetable was served by every other train down the line giving it a service roughly every two hours. Trains ran back towards Newstead and the bigger town of Wilthorpe (where I had previously lived) in one direction, and in the other direction towards Salthaven on the coast. Towards the station I could see a new housing development taking shape, clearly aimed at those who might hanker for the country life yet work in Wilthorpe or Elchester. "A new gated development of six four-bedroomed homes," proclaimed the billboard.

The chalkboard on the wall outside the pub declared two courses for £10.95, three for £12.95. Maybe, on another day I'd sample these culinary delights. I continued past the twenty or so houses that constituted this part of the village. Although this was the main road, it was hardly busy, not even deserving the status of B-Road. Despite the cold, northerly wind, the walk was pleasant enough. After ten more minutes I turned a corner and came to another part of the village, at the end of which, according to the map, I would find the church. Here the well-kept cottages and bigger houses gave the village an elysian and also an affluent feel. Very gratifying was the sight of a village store, a quaint white building covered in weather-boarding. I bought a bottle of water, for I was thirsty, and an unhealthy amount of tea which I am sure drew an amused look from the Miss Marple-esque lady behind the till and took myself to the churchyard. This was clearly the oldest part of the village, whereas that near the station had clearly developed with the arrival of the railway.

The church was impressive, a large square tower in the centre of two red-tiled steeply sloping roofs which must have housed the chancel and the nave. The sign outside indicated it was founded as a place of worship in 1056 although the present flint structure was of a much later, yet still quite ancient, date. On the edge of a large graveyard was a smaller flint structure which might have once been some sort of chapel. Rabbits darted about nibbling the grass, oblivious to the cold. The small juveniles looked particularly endearing. Two collared doves sat on the castellations atop of the tower cooing their monotonous call. Somewhere in a nearby tree a woodpecker cackled although I couldn't see him. I tried the church door, which was, predictably, locked, and I wandered amongst the old stones, awed by the sense of history in this one place. The carved names, some of them illegible, told the brief biographies of lives now almost, if not completely, forgotten. Here lies Elizabeth, sister of so-and-so, Mary, wife of Lord etc: all once persons of mind, conscience and soul (if you believe in such things) but now nothing more than fertiliser for the rabbits' food, and an etched name covered in lichen: a humbling thought. Perhaps Elizabeth or Mary still existed as a painting on a wall in the local grand house or an old sepia photograph rotting slowly in an album in a neglected attic corner, but probably not even that. Luckily my depressive reverie was disturbed by a short burst of sunshine through the clouds, which the wind was now dispersing. I telepathically said goodbye to Florence Weston, wife of George, lost forever after a tragic accident (according to her gravestone), and walked back through the churchyard to the road, past the village shop and back towards the pub and the station.

Ambling home across the fields lifted my mood further. The sun was now shining more often than not, although it was still cold and I was glad of my fleece and hat. Flashes of green and yellow proved to be small birds darting between the hedgerows looking for nest material, too quick to identify. Different bird songs filled the air but the competing sounds never jarred, simply forming a kind of spring symphony of joy and renewed life. At one point the grass beside me seemed to wriggle with life and I watched as a mole scuttled about and then made surprising haste across the path and into the field. It had a soft dark grey fur and a small tail about an inch long. I hoped he would burrow quickly, otherwise he'd make a nice lunch for the kestrel I had just spotted poised in the firmament above. My thoughts drifted smugly to my old colleagues, too busy worrying about school inspectors, assessments and parents' evenings to enjoy a good walk, instead being cooped up in a stuffy classroom or fighting to keep awake in another tedious staff meeting. "Free at last!" I thought somewhat ethereally.

As I approached the house down the lane I felt hungry and began to regret not pausing at the pub to sample their lunches. After all, I would only have to listen to Ray bashing, banging and drilling for the afternoon. A movement in the upstairs window revealed that he must still be fitting the bedroom radiators, so I was surprised to find him in the downstairs back room when I walked in.

"How's it going?" I asked.

"Should be done about five," was the answer. Ray was a man of few words.

I fixed some lunch (toast and marmite, followed by an apple and a banana), and having ascertained that Ray had finished upstairs went up to finally furnish my bedroom. First I swept the floor and cleared it of the saw-dust, metal filings and chalk markings that Ray had left. The walls were now all dry and the smell of paint had almost vanished so I re-constructed the pine bed that had been in pieces on the floor in the front bedroom and set up a bedside table. A bookshelf and a small chest of drawers sufficed in the alcoves either side of the chimney breast. Next I found a lamp for the bedside table, some pictures for the walls, the odd treasured ornament from a fondly remembered holiday and some favourite books, mainly travel related. A Greek vase, a memento of a school expedition to Rhodes, sat nicely on the bookshelf. There was no room for a wardrobe, so I would store all my clothes in the front bedroom, which could fit a guest bed and a wardrobe, as well as having a cupboard built into the space above the stairs. That reminded me, it was Tuesday and I'd be having my first guest to stay on Friday, so I set about cleaning the front bedroom as well. Again, I swept and washed the floor which wasn't in such a good state of repair as the back room. Painting the walls could wait until later and another, less favourite, rug would do instead of a carpet. A couple of pictures went on the walls (one an old print of Elchester Cathedral, a graduation gift from my parents), and I hid all the half-empty boxes in the built-in cupboard, which made the room quite presentable. It is amazing how dressing a room with a few familiar things can transform it. I began to feel less like an alien intruder and was less conscious of the house merely existing around me, uncolonised and stark. Breathing new life into these walled spaces was another chapter for the house too. The front bedroom was now definitely habitable, and I looked forward to showing it all to Sarah when she arrived on Friday night. The spare bed was quite comfortable for a couple of nights. I just needed to dust away the remaining cobwebs and oil the squeaky door.

CHAPTER 5

On Wednesday I decided to brave the attic. It was another cool day, but dry with intermittent sunshine, slowly improving towards the afternoon (or so promised the weatherman on the radio). I had slept remarkably well in my new room, glad for the comforts of my familiar bed, and was surprised not to wake up till nearly seven. I got together a few boxes of bits that I wanted to store up in the roof space and positioned the step ladder. The loft hatch was a small opening in the ceiling in the back bedroom. Hoisting myself up from the ladder, with a torch already switched on and stuffed into my back pocket, I eased in, perching my bottom on the rim of the opening to get my bearings and look about before raising myself up further. The roof rose steeply enough to create plenty of space to stand up in. It was not properly boarded over, but someone had strategically placed hardboard over the beams, sturdy enough to make walking about possible, so long as you were careful where you put your feet. The space was empty and I needn't have worried about clearing out loads of old debris and forgotten stuff. All that remained from the house's previous life were a few old bits of timber, good for nothing except as firewood. There was plenty of dust and a smell of wood stain but no indication of any holes in the roof or rain getting in. It was too early in the year for wasps, but there was plenty of evidence of previous colonies hanging from the beams. In a month's time I'd just check that no new nests were under construction. The idea of being barred from my own loft space by an angry swarm did not appeal: my love of nature stopped short of stinging insects. With very little to investigate, I lowered myself back down the ladder to start lifting the boxes up towards the rim of the opening. Then it was simply a matter of neatly positioning them on the various bits of board so that they were away from the opening but still easy to reach should the need arise in the future.

Shifting the last couple into place, there was a noise behind me. It was distinct from the sound of my own breathing and the sliding of cardboard over a dusty surface. It sounded like a stone landing on the make-shift floor. I froze unconsciously, held my breath and felt the hairs on my arms tingling slightly. The feeling was over in less than a second and I breathed out and turned around. As expected, there was no one there. The notion of not being alone had vanished, but its shadow still fluttered in my mind. Standing up to walk back to the hatch-opening, I did indeed spot a small object near the edge of one of the pieces of hardboard a couple of feet away from where I had been crouching down. I picked it up and dropped it again to see if I could replicate the sound. The noise was close on identical, so I surmised that this piece of brick had fallen onto the hardboard, disturbed by my activity, yet it was not obvious from where it had fallen. Immediately above it there were only wooden beams and roof tiles. Bending down to pick up the piece of brick once more, my eyes noticed a glistening. Something beneath the next piece of hardboard was caught in the beam of the torch. I knelt down to investigate and slowly lifted the board. It was an old tin, the sort my mother or grandmother had years ago to store tea or biscuits in. It was a burnished bronze colour, much tarnished with age. On the lid was a fading picture of a girl dressed in lots of frills and petticoats, Edwardian style. Prizing open the lid I saw a piece of pink note paper folded a couple of times to fit inside the tin, blank except for a small purple iris-type flower in the top centre, and merely there to protect, or hide, what lay below. Lifting this out revealed a small pack of what appeared to be very old hand-written letters; all neatly folded up; some in envelopes, but most without. The envelopes showed no address and no stamp and were simply blank.

Back downstairs, with a cup of tea on the coffee table, it was time to study this secret cache of letters further. There were around twenty or so, all on scraps of paper yellowing with age, written in the same slightly immature looking hand. That did not mean they were composed by a child, since they could have come from a time when people were less literate than now. I did not definitely know they were old - after all none of the letters were dated - but there was something about the feel of the paper, slightly mottled and coarse, and the old tin, that seemed to age them. Even to my untrained eye, they appeared to belong to a time before my own. How old, beyond that, I could only guess.

The letters were all of the same nature:

"I cannot wait until the next time I see you," ran one. "I just want to have you again in my arms. Will let you know when somehow."

"What I want to do to you I can't say," said another, "but I can't bare (sic) the thought of you being stuck there like that when you should be with me. One day, my love, one day soon."

Or more simply, "usual place 2.15".

There were few details, no names, no "Dear..." and no signatures: the briefest of love letters, quick assignations to meet, the place always undisclosed. Whether it was the juvenile handwriting, or whether it was the stereotypical notion that only a woman would keep such frivolous notes, I felt that the author of the letters must have been a man, probably rather uneducated, and probably local (all the letters appeared informally delivered, as if by hand).

My investigation must have lasted all of ten to fifteen minutes. I was partly impressed at the thought of handling something so private, so treasured and so old, and partly disappointed that these old missives revealed so little information about the correspondents. Even if I had known the names of any of the previous occupants of my new home, matching them to the recipient of these letters would be little more than conjecture. Nonetheless, they were a window on the past and a tiny piece of the history of the house. Having touched the letters like they were old heirlooms from a museum archive, out of some unconscious respect for the past, I carefully re-folded them back into the tin, and gazed vacantly at the twee image on the lid as I closed it. Lost in thought, I became aware of feeling cold, and the knot in my stomach reminded me of that sensation I always used to get at the start of a new term, anxious and disquieted. Putting the tin on the bookshelf in the front room, I went through to the kitchen and distracted myself by washing up yesterday's dirty dishes, gazing out at the sky searching for any hint of blue and a return of the warmer weather. I switched on my new heating system to get rid of the chill, as well as give it a good test run, and spent the rest of the morning scrubbing the old bathroom, which was at the back of the house, downstairs, next to the kitchen. My efforts made hardly any impact. The hideous old white bath and 1930s porcelain sink remained green where the drips of decades had left unsightly stains, despite bleach and descaler aplenty. But, appearances aside, I knew it was clean and something more aesthetically pleasing would have to wait for the arrival of a new bathroom.

That afternoon, the weather still being uninviting, I stretched out on an armchair with a good book but soon dozed off, relaxing at last, and still feeling smug about no longer being at work. The heat of the new radiators must have deepened, as well as hastened, my slumber. I was surprised to wake up at a quarter to five, feeling stuffy and stiff, with a dull headache looming. I downed a pint of water, and then brewed a large tea. At least the heating worked properly, and a check that all the radiators were on and not leaking was no doubt prudent. A quick tour of the house revealed that all were working fine, although the front room downstairs still felt strangely chilly. The tin of letters, I noticed, had sprung open and the top two had spilled out onto the floor. I did not like them being here in my living space; not that they were invading my privacy, but more the feeling that *I* had encroached upon them. It might sound like a cliché, but as well as being a window on the past, they also felt like eyes following me reproachfully around the room. So, a quick decision, and I swept them back upstairs, got out the step-ladder, re opened the hatch, and pushed them back into the loft; hopefully out of *their* sight and *my* mind.

Going outside to clear my head, I stood at the open gate at the top of the steps and watched a couple of early evening trains rattle past. The clouds were breaking as the sun fell lower in the sky and the evening was going to be the best part of the day. A sudden craving for fish and chips spurred me into action. I shut the gate, locked up the house, jumped into the car and drove into Newstead in search of a chippy. *Ollie's Fish Bar* seemed to fulfil my requirements, so I spent a pleasant half an hour wandering around the town centre licking the salt and vinegar off my finger tips. It was much quieter this time. The cafes were shut and no one was window shopping. Being a Wednesday, the restaurants and pubs were quiet. A few people wandered homeward with white polythene bags filled with aluminium tubs containing take-away dinners, to be eaten, no doubt, goggling at the one-eyed monster in the corner of the living room. The car park was almost empty as I returned to the car, and dusk began to fall as I drove home.

After spending some time reading and unpacking a few boxes of books in the downstairs front room, I took a long, relaxing soak in the bath and went to bed. However, tonight sleep would not come. I read a bit, and then just lay there, listening to the trains chatter past every half an hour or so. This noise did not upset me, even though the house shuddered slightly as one went past. I had heard somewhere that the sound of a train had always signalled the end of bombing raids during The Blitz, and that the distant rumble of a train had entered the British psyche as a kind of "all is O.K. again" chant, coaxing us into a feeling that we were now out of danger.

Ten to twelve; the final train clattered away, back towards the city. Still I lay there, calm and thoughtful, not tired at all. The bedside clock silently shone the minutes to midnight, and then, the minutes afterwards, those of the new day. Downstairs the wall clock ticked softly as the seconds passed. It was no good, I would have to get up. My afternoon sleep had left me feeling wide awake. I pulled on some jeans and a pair of socks, a T-shirt and a fleece, then finally my trainers and a woolly hat. I crept downstairs and through the kitchen. I unlocked the back door and stepped into the garden. The moon was bright and almost full, so I had no need for the torch in my pocket. There was no wind and the trees and shrubs were now dappled in a metallic blue. Brilliant stars twinkled deeply in the northern sky furthest away from the setting moon. The gate was obstinately open, beckoning me through it. I went down those four, now familiar stone steps and stood on the grey ballast lining the two tracks.

"Let's walk the line a bit," my inner devil said to me, keen to soften the deed by pluralising the participant. Yes, it was illegal and, yes, it was dangerous, but the timetable clearly stated that there were no more trains until twenty-to-six. Obviously, an overnight freight was not out of the question, but I knew enough to be confident that it was many years since the harbour at Salthaven had sent any goods other than passengers down this line. To be safe, I would walk on the right hand track, so as to face any oncoming trains if they approached. I turned east and walked in the direction which the workmen had come from on Sunday. There was something rebellious about breaking the law in this way, even though I felt quite safe. The trains along here were all diesel and there was no live rail, such as you get in some parts of the country. With no one about to hear my feet crunching on the stones, I walked on further, increasing in confidence with every step, gradually rounding the corner that took me out of sight of my own house and into new, but forbidden, territory. The vegetation on either side of the tracks grew thicker and taller as I realised that the line was slowly entering a cutting, the banks lifting to my left and right like two great curtains enclosing me in this long ribbon-like space. Five more minutes and, as expected the hillside in front of me loomed upwards completely blocking my way, except of course, for the gaping mouth of the tunnel entrance, massive, dark and portentous. My footsteps slowed until I stood at the very entrance, on that edge between inside and out as if on the precipice of some great cliff, before some great unknown. It is difficult to explain how I felt. Not scared, not exhilarated, but perhaps somewhere between the two. Being somewhere I had no right to be felt uncomfortable, yet as I looked up at the hollow blackness I felt a sense of awe and wonder for its size, its mystery and its might. It was, after all, built by human hands in the days before heavy machinery and precision engineering. The round entrance itself was framed by large flagstones giving it the appearance of the gateway to a giant, old medieval castle, the tracks like a drawbridge pulling you inside.

Time to go back. I might be foolish enough to wander a railway at night, but I was not entering a tunnel, the end of which could not be seen probably even in daylight. I switched tracks and walked back the way I had come. After only ten minutes, I was at the bottom of the steps again, outside my own garden gate, although the unorthodox nature of this little walk meant that it felt like I had been out on my stroll for much longer. Closing the garden gate behind me, I walked back inside, locked the door and went up to bed. Sleep came much quicker now, the fresh air, and the exhilaration of my walk making me tired. I'm sure I dreamt of railway tunnels that changed into long, serpentine beasts devouring me whole.

CHAPTER 6

Thursday. I am a creature of custom, yet love my new life without an alarm clock. I'm still waking before seven and my first act of the day is to make a cup of tea. I love tea; all types of tea; green tea, black tea, tea with milk, tea without. An old university friend once christened me *Tea-Belly* and the name stuck for a while. In my world the Garden of Eden was a tea plantation and Adam used to dive into a bottomless lagoon full of it.

I take the tea (it's in one of those large pint mugs) back to bed and start to plan the day. Some sort of routine in my life is necessary after years of obeying school bells and timetables. I am missing having a shower and must get one installed over the bath. I don't know whether to wait until I get the whole bathroom done, or just fit a temporary stand-in until I can be bothered to go through the rigmarole of choosing, buying and then getting someone to install a new suite. I might be up to fixing a shower head from the taps to the wall, but my D.I.Y skills won't stretch to tiling and installing an entire new bathroom.

Since joining a gym is not really my thing, before dressing I force myself to do forty press-ups and forty sit-ups, Then it's breakfast (usually yoghurt or cereal) and more tea. The only exception to this, today, was a frustrating search for my watch, which I was sure I had left in the bathroom the evening before.

The memory of my night-time walk still lingering, I set about clearing the garden of some of the errant weeds and shrubs, filling black sack after black sack with waste. The clement weather had returned and as the sun climbed higher, I had to go in and change into a pair of shorts. It was warm work and my hands got sweaty inside the thick gardening gloves which the nettles and brambles forced me to wear. Even so, I was stung and scratched several times. When it was time for my morning coffee, I opened the gate to sit at the top of the steps, where I could enjoy the sunshine. There at the bottom of the steps, on the edge of the ballast was my missing watch. It must have fallen off during my walk, although I was almost certain that I hadn't bothered to put it on again as I went out last night. Was this another strange occurrence or was it just one more example of my absent-mindedness?

Bored with gardening by lunchtime, and after a quick bagel with cheese, I set out on another walk. It was such a nice day that I almost decided to cycle instead, but I hadn't yet pumped up the tyres or oiled the chain. Besides I wanted to explore what, if anything, remained of the old farm buildings down the lane that had once run across the tracks at the old crossing. Picking my moment carefully, I slipped across the tracks and over the fence. A kind of a space led between two hedgerows where the lane had once gone, but it was more overgrown than my back garden. Hoverflies buzzed expectantly and bluebottles zipped in and out of the bushes, animated by ebullient beams of sunshine. It was heavy going and after a particularly vicious thorn bush tore my arm through my T-shirt, I considered heading back. As I swore, and rubbed my arm, I noticed a car driving down an unseen road on the other side of the field beyond the hedge. Pushing myself around a hawthorn bush, my feet stood on a much harder, flatter surface which may well have been the only remains of the old farm buildings to which my lane had once led. A lizard basking on an old piece of exposed concrete darted away and I made my way around the edge of the field to the road.

This was the road that must lead back towards the village. I remembered a crossroads between the pub and the main part of the village. Buoyed by the absence of spiteful thorns, I turned right, revelling in the sunshine and once again thankful that I was no longer ensnared by classroom walls. I had no notion of ever returning to that bureaucratic hell again. A swallow perched on the telegraph wires beside the road, the first I'd seen this year, and an early arrival for certain. Rabbits hopped about in the fields undisturbed by my silent tread. Now and then, one stopped to stare at me, nibbling a thread of grass. Trees wore a vivid coat of green, not yet a fortnight old, joyfully heralding the onset of better weather. As I walked, there was not a sound of a human being, only the murmur of insects and crying of birds. After about half an hour, the revving of a train indicated that I was about to walk beneath a bridge under the railway and I was indeed near to Poppington Station. I caught the sun glinting on the metals of the line overhead. Instead of turning right to head back home, I decided to venture back to the village shop to pick up a few bits in readiness for Sarah's visit tomorrow.

Miss Marple was more chatty this time and, as I put my wire basket down on the counter, she asked me if I was new to the village (she clearly remembered me from the time before).

"I've just moved into the old crossing-gates cottage down by the railway."

"I heard that someone had bought it, at last," she said. "It's been on the market for nearly a year. How are you finding it?"

"Oh I love it," I replied.

"Not too isolated, I hope?"

I grinned. "No."

"Where were you before?"

"Wilthorpe," I said, "just outside Elchester."

"Well I hope you'll be very happy here." She smiled and placed my groceries inside the plastic bag, offering me the handles as she took my money.

"See you again soon," I smiled back, taking my change, and heading for home.

*

The following day Sarah texted at about five saying she was then leaving work, and should be with me in just over an hour. It had been another glorious day, and I had spent most of it outdoors clearing more of the garden and was pleased to have created enough space for my small garden table and a couple of chairs. Before a cleansing bath, I put a bottle of wine in the fridge.

I had first met Sarah nearly twenty years ago when we started working at Longfields Secondary School and Sixth Form College, both fresh out of teacher training. She taught Science and both of us became firm comrades as the pair of newbies down at the pub after lessons on a Friday. She had tired of teaching before me, and left after about seven years to switch career, working for an agrochemical firm the other side of Elchester, thanks to a contact she made via her sister. I left Longfields a year later to become Head of Department at West Riverside, a private school in a leafy suburb between Wilthorpe and Elchester, but we stayed in touch and still met every couple of months or so, at mine or hers, for a weekend of wine and reminiscing. There had been a brief time when I thought our friendship might have been heading towards something deeper, but I never felt the feelings were reciprocated, and then, of course, she met Craig.

For a while, I saw her less. She was all loved-up, and when I met someone too, we were definitely beyond that point of ever becoming a couple. I realised that, although I enjoyed her company, she was not the one for me.

The thing with Craig came to a bitter and sorry end (Sarah came off much the worse) and I too found myself single again, but the friendship had survived and was probably better and stronger for it.

At twenty past six I heard the crunch of car tyres on the gravel outside shortly followed by a loud knock.

"Sarah! Come on in!" I said, flinging open the door.

"Ed! You look fabulous too darling!" she quipped, arms outstretched, a bottle of wine in each hand, and a beaming smile across her face. "I'd never have found this if your directions hadn't been so good! It's in the middle of nowhere!"

"Well? What d'you think?"

"It's marvellous! Let me put these two down and you can show me round."

I fetched her bag from outside, and gave her another hug. "Cup of tea, or something stronger?"

"I'm dying for a cuppa. Tea first while you show me around, then we'll open the wine for a natter."

I took her through to the kitchen and she squealed with delight. "All your things but in somewhere so different!"

"It's going to need a bit of work to get it ship-shape," I said, half apologising, "but I really *do* love it."

A train rumbled past noisily, and the mugs rattled on the kitchen work top. "I can see why! Those trains are really close. Let me have a look!" Sarah knew me well enough to know all about my love for trains. She made straight through the back door whilst I followed with the teas. Outside,

Sarah sighed deeply and took a good look around.

"You've caught the sun," she said, finally turning to face me.

"Yes I've been out here most of today and my shoulders are tingling a bit."

I showed her around the small garden and Sarah named a few of the plants that I'd been unable to identify. "These'll be crocosmia, I think... And this looks like a wild strawberry plant." She admired the gate and we stood by the steps leading down to the trackside. "This is perfect for you. Now you can watch the trains go by every day!"

The tour of the house did not take long, and good old Sarah said all the right things, encouraging and enthusiastic about the size of the rooms, the views from the windows, the exposed floorboards and the open fire places. She didn't launch into a homily of *you could do this in this room* or *you should knock down that wall*, as some of my friends would. She greeted everything with a child-like rapture and was full of questions.

We went back outside with the bottle of wine from the fridge, a corkscrew and a couple of glasses. "Here's to your new home," she said raising her glass for the first taste.

"My new home and my new life," I replied

"How does it feel to have finally left teaching?"

"Amazing! I've retired to the country at last!"

"You're a bit young to be 'retired' aren't you? More like having a few years off."

"Sarah, I'm forty-three, I've taught in two high-pressured schools for twenty years and I'm exhausted with it. I've got no dependants and no kids to support through university. Why should I work until I'm pushing sixty-five, so knackered that I drop down dead of a heart attack? Besides, the job was no longer what it was when we started. It wasn't about the students any more, just about exam grades. I felt like a machine in an exam factory, spewing out ever-higher grades, year after year, always being told to do even better."

"And not missing your modern *des res* in Wilthorpe, then?"

"It served its purpose, in that it was handy for work, and buying it when I did was the investment that meant I could sell up and buy this place outright, mortgage free. I've set aside enough cash to get a new kitchen and bathroom. But that *Avenue Green Estate* was a soulless Legoland of manicured front lawns and an Audi on every driveway; all the houses so tightly confined that everyone's garden was overlooked by at least five other houses. Here, at least, I've got the best sort of 'lonely', with no stuffy neighbours tutting every time my brother's kids come over and want to play football in the back garden."

"So what are you going to *do* all day?" Sarah asked.

"Lots of walks, bike rides and chilling," I smiled. "Maybe I'll even write a book!"

"And, if you don't mind me asking, what will you do for money? Or did you *really* make a fortune selling your last place?"

"I've got enough to keep me going for about a year, if I'm frugal. I want to try exam marking. They're always crying out for people to mark 'A' Levels and GCSEs."

"Good for you!" Sarah cried, chinking my glass,

downing her drink and helping herself to another. "Hmm. This is nice! It's not one of the ones I brought is it? Where d'you get it?"

And this led to me describing the village, the shop, the church and the local countryside. We sat there chatting for about half an hour trying to absorb the dying rays of the sun, but then it turned chilly so we took our glasses indoors and I set about cooking the pasta. (It is amazing what you can do with just a microwave and an old gas ring.)

As we ate and opened the next bottle of wine, Sarah spoke of her job and how she was awaiting the next round of redundancies since her firm had been taken over by the Americans, which, the way she felt at the moment would be a blessing in disguise. Since losing her mother last summer she had no desire to stay, and had almost talked herself into leaving anyway to spend some time in Australia with her brother.

Finally, as usual, we fell to reminiscing about Longfields; how the old head teacher there had always reminded us of Leslie Crowther, and how two P.E. teachers had been caught in a compromising position in the gym cupboard. Sarah brought up a particularly awful school trip to Alton Towers where five students had disgraced themselves by mooning out of the back window of the coach, the memory of which soon had us in uncontrollable fits of laughter.

All in all, a most refreshing evening. Finally, Sarah said, it was time for her to go to bed. Both of us were starting to yawn, so I found her a fresh towel and showed her to her room.

CHAPTER 7

Two pints of water and a similar amount of tea helped dull the headache I awoke with. Sarah was able to sleep in longer and came down, just before ten, as bright as a button. We both breakfasted on sausage, egg, bacon and baked beans, then retired outside and sat in the sun with a morning coffee.

"Did you sleep all right?" I asked.

"Like a log," she replied, adding that she'd had to put socks on because her feet were cold.

After about half an hour, I suggested a drive into Newstead, and Sarah, ever keen for an excuse to shop, was more than happy. Saturday, we were delighted to find, was market day. This meant finding a parking space took ten minutes of circling aimlessly until we lucked upon someone just leaving. The market was set out in a large square in the centre of town, which tapered off at one end down a wide street towards the Guildhall. It was a colourful affair, many of the stalls decked out beautifully, the traders keen to cash in on the glorious weather, which had undoubtedly lured the locals out of doors. One stall sold cut price, near-its-sell-by-date groceries, so I stocked up on crisps, biscuits, a few pickles and even a jar of olives. At the plant stall we bought a few herbs and a couple of small conifers for my garden. A second-hand DVD stall gave us four films that we'd never got round to seeing when they first came out. Finally, I stocked up on fruit and veg, to save a trip to the supermarket. Sarah was thrilled to find a small shop devoted to hats and bags, and after deliberating for twenty minutes over two bags, bought both. A real find was a bric-a-brac shop called *Aladdin's Junk Emporium* where Sarah spotted a large iron-framed mirror that would go perfectly in my downstairs back room. Leaving all our purchases in the car, we returned to a little lane just off the market place and had a late lunch in a small hidden restaurant, which we would have been unable to get into had we arrived any earlier. I enjoyed a lamb and date tagine, and Sarah had a creamy fish dish in a nest of fried potatoes. It was the sort of restaurant you congratulate yourself on finding, vowing to bring other visitors there on the next occasion.

The rest of the day was spent back at the house, first arranging where the new plants would go in the garden, then hanging the mirror in the back downstairs room, grateful to have a second person to tell me where it did, or did not, look right. Sarah had been correct: it suited the back room impeccably, reflecting the light from the window back towards the darkest corners. The iron framework somehow seemed to go with the house. The two large rooms downstairs replicated the two bedrooms upstairs, and as I got used to living in the new house, I found I was gravitating towards living more in the back room, where I had put my table and an old easy chair. The staircase divided the two rooms, allowing for a nice alcove under the stairs. With Sarah to chat to, we mainly sat in the front room where I had an armchair and a small sofa, but I knew that when I was on my own, I'd be living much more in the rear of the house, which seemed cosier, and was, of course, the centre of the house. Off this was the kitchen, through which was a small utility room, containing the back door to the garden and a small cupboard, barely large enough to hold a few spare plant pots. The bathroom was beyond this and the whole of this section of the house jutted out into the back garden a single storey "extension" to the main part of the house, although still part of the original building as far as I could tell.

Sarah and I chatted away well into the evening. As the light faded, she became more serious, speaking for a while of her mother and then about Craig. Two very different wounds, she said, that were still taking their time to heal. We drank no wine that second evening, and headed for bed around eleven. The day had been warm, but this was still April and the evenings grew cool quickly.

Sarah was to leave on Sunday after lunch, so we had decided to take a morning walk across the fields in the direction of the village. However, our departure was delayed by Sarah being unable to locate one of her shoes. I searched downstairs, while she went through all her stuff upstairs, emptying her bag to see if she'd put it in there by mistake. Five minutes is a long time to search for something that really can't have gone far, and eventually I stopped short during my second scour of the bathroom. I stood up straight, opened the back door and strode out into the garden. It didn't surprise me that the gate was open, and, just as I dreaded, there at the bottom of the steps was one brown shoe.

I picked it up, almost angrily, and strode back indoors, still unsure what I would tell Sarah.

"Found it!" I yelled up the stairs.

"At last! Wherever was it?"

She came down the stairs putting her cardigan on as she descended. "Where was it?" she repeated, as if I hadn't heard her.

"I'll show you," I replied and led her into the back garden. I pointed through the gateway and said, "Down there at the bottom of the steps."

"Well how did it get there?" She looked blankly, first at the steps, then at me, then again at the steps, wondering if this was some sort of joke. I was saved from answering immediately by the sudden hum of the rails which always preceded an approaching train. The boisterous clamour of the train rushing past with its raucous underfloor diesel engines seemed to reply for me. As quickly as it came, the sound dimmed and faded, until it was superseded by that slight hum again. Then there was just the benign sound of birds and insects in the genial country air.

"Let's go for our walk," I said, perhaps rather curtly. Sarah said nothing.

We went back through the garden and locked

the back door, before setting off, up the lane from the front of the house.

After about a minute, Sarah said, "*Well...?*"

"*Well*-what?"

"Are you going to tell me what's the matter?"

"Yes... but..." I paused, "It's going to sound a bit odd."

"What do you mean?"

"Your shoe isn't the first thing that's vanished and reappeared on those steps. My keys have turned up there; so has my watch; and even the bloke who came to fit the new boiler, his tape measure ended up there too. My keys and watch, I put that down to me dropping them when I was out there, but the tape measure and your shoe just don't make sense... And another thing, the gate often seems to open by itself. It takes a bit of a shove to open and shut it, and before I moved in, it appeared to be permanently jammed. I could never open it whilst viewing the house. But once I moved in it was just open. And now it seems to open all the time of its own accord."

"It sounds like you're saying there's something spooky going on. Is that what you mean?"

"Yes, it does sound like that, but I don't believe in ghosts or hauntings."

"No..." She sounded uncertain.

We walked on silently for a few moments. Then I said, "I'm open to the idea that there are things that we can't explain: energies and the like. It impressed me when someone once said that radio waves always existed, even before we discovered them. Once we had discovered them, the idea of music or voices being transmitted invisibly through the air became common-place, but before that discovery such things would have been a mystery."

"You're sounding philosophical, but what you really mean is that these things moving by themselves must have a rational explanation, you just don't know what it is yet."

"Hmm," I agreed, thoughtfully.

Sarah continued; "It's just possible that you dropped your watch and keys. Maybe the boiler man did go outside. Did you watch him all the time? The gate's probably opening because you've been using it and the wood has shrunk in all this warm weather. As for my shoe, well that's harder because one was upstairs and the other was outside. Maybe one of us sleep-walks and took it out in the night? A fox or a dog could have got in whilst we weren't looking and carried the shoe outside. We have been leaving the back door wide open."

"These don't seem very likely explanations," I countered.

"But you can't think of a better one?"

"No, to be honest, I can't."

Sarah laughed, "Well if you are being haunted, I'll be back to check it out! You're not scared are you? Being on your own, in the middle of nowhere like this. Your mind will easily play tricks on you, you know. I think you're just getting used to living in such a different place."

"And your shoes?"

"Ed, if I had a fiver for each time I'd lost something and it turned up later somewhere else, I'd be rich. I'm such a dozy cow at times, I'd lose my head if it wasn't screwed on," she laughed.

We carried on walking along the footpath and eventually came out on the lane near the station, walking back via the road. The weather was, yet again, most kind, and this being the first day of May, the sunshine felt quite strong out of the cool breeze. I put thoughts of the unexplained movements of objects to the back of my mind and concentrated on enjoying Sarah's company for the short time that she remained. I wasn't convinced about the fox or the sleep-walking, but what she'd said about the warm weather shrinking the wooden gate and causing it to open made sense.

Once we'd got home and had a quick and simple lunch, I arranged to meet up with Sarah again in a couple of weekends time. After we hugged outside the front door, she threw her bag on the back seat, climbed in and said, "Well, Ed, I love the house, and I'm dead jealous that I've got to go to work on Tuesday and you haven't. See you in two weeks. Come to mine if you miss the city lights, but I'm more than happy to return here again. It's been so relaxing; like a retreat. And I'll probably want to go back to that nice bag shop in town again! Take care!" By now she had put on her seatbelt, rolled down the window and switched on the ignition.

"Bye!" I called as her car eased away.

"Bye," she replied. "Ring me if you see any ghosts!" and with that her car disappeared down the lane.

CHAPTER 8

With Sarah gone, the house felt empty again, so to keep myself occupied, I gave my mountain bike a brief service. After oiling the chain and pumping up the tyres it was ready for use. So, the following day starting sumptuously without a cloud in the sky, I began to explore further afield on two wheels.

The cold of the night was swiftly vanquished in the May sunshine and I took a route east: across some quiet country lanes and bridleways, discovering cottages and hamlets, farmsteads and quaint churches: altogether charming images of a rural idyll and a sense that time had forgotten such a quilted picture of cosy England. I stopped for a swig of water after half an hour outside a farm gate. A giant barn creaked gently as it warmed up. Somewhere nearby a cockerel was crooning. A couple of buzzards pewed overhead, circling higher and higher on the gathering thermals. I urged myself to continue pedalling, even on reaching a very long, arduous hill, pausing for another rest only at the summit. I gazed at the view of rolling greens and yellows, as the hedgerows and fields dipped into shallow valleys, and clumps of trees sat like crests upon the static waves. Polythene tunnels, probably full of strawberries and other soft fruits, glimmered like vast lakes in the distance. A silent moving line of blue betrayed where the railway lay and, although I couldn't see it, I could just about work out where my house would be. Nestling further down the line, I could make out the tower of Poppington Church and after a quick check of the map, and another sip of water, I set off in this direction feeling comfortably cooler as I free-wheeled down hill through the morning air.

On reaching the village, I popped into the shop for some more provisions and a few bits for my lunch. I was surprised to see a group of children outside as I was unlocking my bike, and realised that it was the Bank Holiday, which answered the question as to why they weren't at school. Funny how I used to look forward to holidays so much whilst I was working, knowing the dates of each one well in advance and counting down towards them. Now I was blissfully unaware of such things.

In fifteen minutes I was home, hungrily eating a hastily made cheese and salad sandwich. I sat in the garden, enjoying the nice weather, while the odd cloud that bubbled up provided a cool relief from the unseasonable heat. As a train grumbled past towards the coast, packed to the seams with day trippers, I thought wryly of all those mad people sitting in traffic jams heading for the beach.

I couldn't sit still for long. My eye caught some bindweed under the lilac and I set about tugging it out, filling yet more bin-bags with other debris and weeds. On the right hand side of the garden, a kind of primitive patio revealed itself, which you would have never known was there before I cleared away all the clumps of grass, nettles and even a thriving bramble bush. Old bottles, mostly plastic, but a couple made of glass, were exposed as I cleared away yet more weeds. Some must have lain there for years since last discarded by someone on the railway, in the days when trains all had opening windows, and passengers flung out rubbish regardless of where it might end up. Ageing drinks cans and shrivelled bits of plastic called to mind how my students used to rib me for taking home their litter to put in my recycling bin.

In one corner of the garden, I began to uncover what I initially thought was a load of useless rubble. Further excavation unveiled what might have once been a rockery, long since bereft of decorative plants. Some of the large stones were quite ornate, so I lifted them across the garden and began to set them aside under the bathroom window. It was warm, sweaty work, but very gratifying. These would be useful to decorate the planned flower-beds.

On bending down to retrieve another, a voice behind me said, "Hello there!"

I stood up and turned round, still holding the rock, to see a woman standing in the garden. She was dressed in a simple, but flattering, dark summer dress, a sun hat and sunglasses.

"Hallo," I replied.

"I hope I didn't startle you, but I couldn't get an answer from the front door, so I wandered round the house to see if you were in the garden. Are you Mr Southern?"

"I am indeed. How can I help you?"

"I have your wallet here." She held out my wallet and I put the large stone down. I could see it was mine before I took it.

"You dropped it outside the village shop," she said, answering my puzzled look. "This morning," she continued, smiling, as she watched my face gradually understand the situation. "Some children handed it in at the shop. Apparently they called after you, but you'd already cycled off and didn't hear them. My mother said you lived here, and as we couldn't ring you, I decided to drop it back in on my way past."

"Your mother?"

"Yes, she owns the shop, and she said that you'd moved in down here." Again, she smiled, taking off her sunglasses. "Sorry, I haven't introduced myself. I'm Belinda Taylor." She held out her hand to shake mine and I suddenly felt embarrassed to be so grubby and covered in garden muck. Hurriedly, I grabbed my T-shirt and pulled it on over my head.

"Well, thank you very much. I'm Ed," I said, wiping my hands on my shirt and finally shaking hers. "Luckily, I hadn't even noticed it was missing. If I had, I'd have been going frantic. I'd be indoors right now phoning the bank, cancelling all my cards. Thank you again. You've saved me a lot of trouble." I paused unsure what to say next, anxious to offer some reward for rescuing me from the torment of no wallet, no cards and no cash. I really was very grateful. "Sorry. Can I offer you a drink or something? Cup of tea?"

"No, thank you, that's very kind. I can see you're busy," she replied, sensing my dilemma. She quickly cast her eye round the garden as if curious about what I had been doing. "I was passing this way anyway, on my way home. I live in Newstead, and I've spent the day visiting my mother. I've had the day off work, with it being the Bank Holiday."

"Do you work in Newstead?" (Why do I always have to ask such dumb questions?)

"Yes, I do, in the library on St Giles' Street."

"Oh. Well, it's nice to meet you. And, thank you again for bringing back the wallet."

"Not at all, and nice to meet you too," she said.

With that she turned, and walked back round the house and out of sight. I stared after her, lost in reverie, and heard her car start up before heading back up the lane. I hate losing things, and my wallet has to be the worst to lose of the lot. How fortunate that I'd been spared the panic of even knowing it was gone, and what providence it was, that I'd been saved from connecting it with all that business concerning the back gate.

*

My bike ride had buoyed me up so much, that I decided on another the following day. I was up before six, and set out just after seven, heading towards a village I'd seen on the map called Goose Hill. In truth, there can be nothing finer than a sunny May morning. It had been a warm night, and today dawned bright and shimmering, full of the hope of halcyon summer days yet to come, along with the shorter and shorter nights. As I cycled, timber-framed houses bobbed into view like holiday scenes on picture-postcards, and soft clouds billowed over the tree tops looking like Alpine peaks gleaming with snow. Cycling isn't nearly as strenuous as the exertion of a run. Torpedoing down hills, the wind in your face, I reckon, resembles swooping through the oceans like a dolphin: always moving on, never arriving: just like that old motto *mobilis in mobili.*

On my way home, at about ten o'clock, I dropped by the village store to give Miss Marple a tenner for the children who had handed in my wallet, assuming they were local. She said they often dropped in and it was a nice gesture: the sort of thing that would encourage them to be honest citizens in the future. I suppose I must stop calling her Miss Marple, now that I have met her daughter, and realise that she is not the solitary old spinster I had imagined her to be.

I spent the afternoon tidying the house. I carried as many bin bags as I thought I could fit into the car round to the front, ready for a trip to the tip tomorrow. I was glad that I rang the council to find out about refuse collections, as it appeared they were unaware that the house was occupied. I cleaned the kitchen and peered under the lino to discover some huge, black flagstones, worthy of a church. I also sorted through the rest of the unopened boxes, before moving those that I had no need of, upstairs into my bedroom, and finally up the step ladder into the loft.

For dinner, I made a passable vegetable stew, vowing once again to get someone round to mend the old cooker. Big news, on the radio, was the current heatwave, since the mercury had hit twenty-five degrees Celsius today, and similar, if not warmer temperatures were forecast for the rest of the week. Sales of barbecue items were "simply flying off the shelves" and traders at the coast were tripling what they had made at the same time last year. Supermarkets were running out of ice-cream, beer, and salad items. Trade at garden centres was brisk. Doctors were advising people to be wary of sunburn: just like every other warm spell in recent British history!

With the washing-up done, and the house tidy, I went upstairs to fetch a book. On noticing a chalk cross, scrawled on the floorboards underneath the loft hatch, I bent down for a closer look. I wondered if the step ladder could have left such a mark on the floor, unlikely as this seemed. I don't know what made me look, but I lifted the blue rug at one corner. There were more chalked crosses, all roughly the same size. Letting the corner of the rug drop back into place, I stood to move the bed a couple of feet, so that I could reveal more of the floor. Under the rug were the boards that I had cleaned just a few days before, and, in all, I counted about sixteen crosses, although these were only the ones I could see. I moved the bed even further to one side, so that I could see the whole floor. The crosses continued. They hadn't been there when I laid the rug, the underside of which I checked, to see if there was something that could have been the cause. Running my hands over the hessian underlay, I detected nothing. What were they? How on earth did they get there? And *why* were they there? Bemused, and somewhat resigned, I added this phenomenon to the others. If this *was* anything supernatural, I was not going to be fazed by it. Objects appearing outside, self-opening gates, and crosses chalked on the floor-boards were not going to scare me. I shrugged, stood up, letting the blue rug fall back into place, and returned the bed to its proper position. Then I remembered the first cross, the week before, which I had thought was due to Ray fitting the radiators. My eye fell upon the piece of brick still laying on the mantelpiece, where I had left it. I had picked this up when I had seen that other cross, again, assuming it had been Ray.

The window was open, so I snatched up the small piece of brick and threw it down into the garden, watching as it thudded, into the grass.

CHAPTER 9

A broken picture greeted me as I came down the following morning. It was a small print of a 1920s poster, *EAST COAST: It's quicker by rail.* Only the glass had smashed, the picture itself would be fine in a new frame. Annoying enough, however, to hoover up all the shards of glass before I could do anything else. The picture hook lay bent by the skirting board, presumably lured out of the wall by the vibrations of a passing train, although I had not woken up when it fell and smashed.

The nearest refuse dump and recycling centre was on my side of Newstead, by the football ground, down an unassuming country lane. The lady at the council had informed me yesterday on the phone that it opened at nine, and I must have been the first caller of the day, as they were still opening the gates as I drove up. As I emptied bag after bag of weeds, I resolved to either compost next time, or have a bonfire.

It had been in the back of my mind for a

couple of days that I would investigate the local library, on St Giles' Street, for the sole purpose of doing some research on the railway that ran past the house. The building was opposite the Post Office, and was a low oblong affair, unremarkable and utilitarian, fronted with red brick and pebbledash. Probably built about forty years ago, it was showing its age, but was unlikely to receive any tender loving care in the near future, in this age of austerity. As I walked in, I scanned the large rectangular room, lined with shelves and racks, making my way towards the rear right-hand corner, where a tall dark-haired lady was deep in conversation with a shorter woman who had tight, brown, wavy hair.

"Hello again," I announced to the taller one, who had looked up as I approached.

"Hello," she said. "Not busy in the garden today?"

"Maybe later," I replied.

Belinda turned to the other lady, who I took to be a colleague. "This is Mr Southern. He's just moved to Poppington, and knows Mum from going to the shop."

The colleague, who reminded me of Imelda Staunton in the Harry Potter films, smirked and said nothing.

"I was wondering if there were any books here about the history of the local railway," I said to Belinda. "Thought I'd do some research."

"Yes, of course, over here." She led me towards the other side of the room into an area surrounded by three shelves, two jutting out perpendicular to the wall. "The transport section is here, but you might fair better in the local history section, which is round the other side." She pointed round the bookcase to the left.

"Thanks," I said.

"Let me know if you need anything," she replied returning in the direction of Imelda.

The transport section revealed some car manuals, an encyclopaedia of trains, a book about airline liveries, and one about the heyday of the local bus company, which appeared to be the 1950s. The local history section contained such gems as the area's windmills, a history of the town's brewery, and the story of the local grammar school.

Returning to the transport section, I discovered a book I had previously missed, due to it being pushed into the shelf spine first. This looked much more like it; *Branch Lines Around Salthaven,* and a quick glimpse showed it covered the line from Elchester to Salthaven, as well as a couple of others along the coast which had closed in the Beeching era. The book was one of a series, the like of which I had seen before, showing a pictorial history of a line, or group of lines, through a selection of old maps and photos.

"Found anything?"

I was so engrossed that I hadn't noticed Belinda returning.

"Yes," I said showing her the book.

We walked over to the desk and I gave my details for membership of the library. As Belinda typed into the computer, I fingered through some leaflets that were in the rack at the end of the counter. Newstead had more to offer than I had realised. There was a local history society, an amateur dramatics association, a gardeners club, a bridge club, the ramblers and an ornithologists group. I took a leaflet detailing plays and exhibitions at the local theatre, which turned out to be beside the swimming pool, although I'd never noticed it. Belinda scanned my book and handed it to me.

"Thanks very much," I said. "Three weeks?"

"That's right, but you can renew over the phone, or online. And don't forget, you can take up to five books at a time. *Use us or lose us*, as they say."

"Well, just this one for now, and the leaflet, thanks," I said. "Oh, and thanks again about my wallet."

"That's ok. It was kind of you to give that money as a reward to the children." Clearly every little action was minutely reported upon in these parts. Perhaps reading my mind, she quickly added, with a coy smile, "My mother mentioned it."

"It was the least I could do." I said, returning the smile. "Bye."

"Bye."

As I walked towards the door, Imelda Staunton was peering round a bookcase at me, quickly busying herself with an imaginary task when she caught my eye.

My trunks were still in the car, so I went for a quick swim (noticing the theatre next-door this time), before heading home. It was late morning when I got back, and I fixed a strong coffee, and retired to the garden to sit in the sun and examine the book.

The pictures, some even dating back to shortly after the railway opened, showed a variety of trains plying the local lines, some careering through the stations at full pelt. Others showed sidings and platforms full of milk churns and other agricultural produce. More fascinating still, were those of people working on the railways, standing stock still in unnatural poses for the camera. The first section began with pictures of the large terminus station in Elchester and followed the line through Wilthorpe, Eastend and then out towards Newstead and Salthaven.

Of great interest to me, naturally, was an old picture of my own cottage, complete with the gates at the old crossing, and a man, presumably the resident crossing keeper, standing on the opposite side of the tracks staring at the camera. The house looked very similar to how it appeared nowadays, but the garden to the left of the gates (which was where I was sitting at this very moment) was far more organised and manicured. A proper railwayman's garden with lines of vegetables, rows of canes and much tamer hedges and shrubs. It had been taken in 1933.

The next picture was taken twenty years later, and was of the entrance to the tunnel where I had trespassed the other night. Amazingly, the caption read: "*The quiet village of Poppington found itself in the national spotlight on Sunday 24th May 1953 after the boat train from London was held up in this tunnel at 01.20, about a quarter of a mile from the previous picture. A wealthy merchant, on his way to Antwerp was murdered, his assailant making away with a considerable treasure of both cut and uncut diamonds. The perpetrator of this terrible act, a local named Robert Wallace, was caught after a police hunt lasting nearly two weeks. He was later tried and executed for his crimes, but the diamonds were never recovered. Poppington Tunnel is over half a mile long, making it the longest between Elchester and Salthaven and emerges shortly before the village station."*

Intrigued by this, I hungrily scoured the pages for further references to this notorious event, to find none whatsoever. Disappointing as this was, I remained engrossed in the old pictures, some of places familiar, now changed to varying degrees, but all images of the past, captured for posterity. What would future generations make of our own media-filled, over-exposed, current way of life? There'd be so much to trawl through, they wouldn't know where to start. Back in the days where cameras were a rarity, old photographs, such as those in the book, somehow seemed more treasured and meaningful.

I put the book back indoors to read later and returned to the garden to dig over an area for planting, possibly inspired by the picture of the garden from 1933. I arranged the large stones around the new bed, to give it a kind of border, and then began to feel my back burning in the strong sunshine, so I retired to the shade with a long cool drink of orange juice diluted with fizzy water. I sat as birds swooped overhead and a couple of trains coasted past. A blue tit visited the nuts I had hung up, before darting into the bushes to eat his prize in secret. To avoid dozing off, I eventually went indoors and took a long relaxing soak in the bath.

I returned to the book that evening after dinner,

and must have sat absorbed for over an hour, so I didn't notice dusk falling and the failing light making reading more of a strain. Resting my eyes, I was on the verge of getting up, when abruptly, a most fearful crash overhead stopped me in my tracks. Unconsciously, I froze, listening for further noise. Nothing: deadly silence. After maybe half a minute, the stillness grew slightly less uncomfortable and I slowly raised myself out of my seat. It already seemed to be darker than a few moments ago, but I didn't switch on the light. I think I wanted be as quiet as possible, the shattering noise still echoing in my ears.

I will confess, I was rather alarmed, and softly climbed the stairs. The house was noiseless around me. I halted at the top of the staircase, listening for any further sounds. I had been reading in the back room downstairs, so it was to the back bedroom that I turned. Knowing I had left the window open, the thought crossed my mind that I might find that a bird had flown in, and was now flapping around in confusion - but I knew at once that I would be able to hear it, if this were the case. Maybe it was dead?

Stepping into the room, I found that the bookcase had tumbled over, most of the books ending up strewn on the floor. The Greek vase, the souvenir from Rhodes, was shattered into several pieces, but there was no sign of life: no bird or cat that had got in through the open window.

I was, at first, upset, then relieved that it hadn't been something more. (What?) On inspecting the top shelf, I saw that it had broken under the burden of the books, their weight gradually weakening, then breaking, the support, until they tumbled off with a force that must have tipped the entire bookcase with them. Unwilling to reflect on the matter any further, I commiserated by gathering the pieces of the broken vase into the largest remaining section and took them downstairs to the kitchen bin.

CHAPTER 10

The following two days were spent enjoying the good weather, casting off across the fields and exploring the various pockets of woodland that I could see from the house, and even a few beyond that. The trees provided welcome shade from the heat, above marine carpets of fresh bluebells.

Life in a school, even an academic one with few discipline problems, had become a claustrophobic experience. Torn between a desire for an easy life and a growing weariness with the monotony of teaching the same thing year after year, you would have thought that the one would have cancelled out the other. Yet it never quite seemed like that. The teaching may have grown easier with time, but the demands of assessment, school inspectors, thinking agendas, memory agendas and recruitment evenings seemed ever greater year on year. The grass had always appeared greener elsewhere, and nowhere more so than a life of idleness, such as I found myself living now.

Longing for the next holiday, was like wishing my life away, and holidays were a battle between the need to rest-and-recuperate and the desire to use every moment to good effect, without wasting a single second. It had been five months since I had left teaching, and the time had been busily spent organising my house move. My arrival here was the end of one chapter, and I hoped, the start of a newer, more positive, one. Yet now I feared that I could no longer be bothered to do very much at all. I kept urging myself to drive to Wilthorpe to order a new kitchen and bathroom, but each day dawned with the sun shining, which just wasn't conducive to my sitting in a stuffy car and dragging myself around the shops.

The evening following the bookcase incident, there was a knock at the door. I was washing up, so it must have been around seven o'clock. I dried my hands and went through to answer it.

"I hope I'm not disturbing you."

It was Belinda. "No, of course not," I said. "Please come in."

She hesitated. "Thanks, but I won't stop. I'm on my way to Mum's, and I just dropped in to give you this, if you wanted it." She held out a small piece of paper, which I took to be a postcard. "It's a ticket to see *The Tempest* on Saturday night, at the theatre in town," she said hurriedly. "It might not be your thing, so don't worry if you don't fancy it. There's a group of us going. I noticed you'd picked up a leaflet about the theatre in the library, and a friend of ours has dropped out, so I was just wondering if, maybe, you'd like it? Please don't feel obliged or anything, its just a spare ticket, and we, I mean 'I', was wondering if you'd like to come?" She stopped and drew breath.

"Thanks," I said. "That's really kind of you, I..."

"Oh you don't have to decide now. I've no idea what the play will be like, or even if its any good. I'm not sure *The Tempest* is one of my favourite Shakespeare's anyway. We're meeting outside at seven fifteen, or at half six in *The Ship,* which is the pub opposite. If you decide you want to come, just turn up."

"That sounds really nice. Thanks. Do you have a mobile number I can text you on, so that you know whether to expect me or not?"

Belinda smiled and gave me the number, whilst I scribbled it down. She seemed happy that she hadn't forced me to do something out of politeness, and even though I felt certain I would go, I just wanted a moment to consider it further. Either that, or I didn't want to come across as quite so eager to please.

Just as she turned to go, she asked, "How was the book?"

"Very interesting," I replied. "I never realised the line behind my house was the scene of a great train robbery in the 1950s."

"No. Neither did I," she replied. "Fancy something as exciting as that happening around here! Well, bye then."

"Bye. And thanks again for the invite."

I closed the door and smiled. I think I had just been asked out on a date. Ten minutes later, I texted to say I'd see her in the pub at about half six.

*

Friday dawned; sublime and golden. After doing my exercises and having some breakfast, I drove off early to Newstead to buy some compost and some plants at the local garden centre. Having dug the planting bed, and surrounded it with the large stones, I was keen to plant it up before the weeds took hold, and the rest of the day was, therefore, spent creating something more of my outside space. The garden was generously proportioned and I would have more than enough room for a couple of flower beds and a vegetable border. I might even try growing some raspberries and other fruits in the sunniest area towards the house. The middle I would leave for a lawn, but couldn't decide whether to make do and mend with the patchy grass that was, or dig it over for re-seeding or re-turfing.

The weather was such that I must have drunk at least a pint of water, and despite putting some sun protection cream on, I could still feel my back burning again in the strong sunshine. After lunch, I sat in a deck chair, proudly surveying my work, watching the trains go by through the open gate. I have no idea where my love for trains ever came from, but my earliest memory is of my father taking me to sit on his lap, in the front seat of the car, watching the trains go past at Higston Junction, just outside Elchester, probably while my mother was at the shops. Clearly a seed had been planted at this early age, and I sometimes regretted not seeking a career on the railways.

I had enjoyed a happy childhood, sharing it with two younger brothers, who came along three and five years after me respectively. As the family had grown we'd moved into a larger property over a hundred miles away near Kingston when my father's job had been relocated, due to a promotion within the construction firm, where he worked. The move coincided nicely with my move from primary to secondary school, and my parents still lived in Kingston to this day. Traditionally, I had always tried to pay them a visit every school holiday, but I was no longer tied by the academic calendar and could visit them now whenever I liked. Both retired, they had no other commitments, and even talked of coming to visit me once I'd got the place more ship-shape. My return to Elchester, after qualifying as a teacher, had been more of a coincidence than a yearning to return to the area of my childhood, but I had chosen well since it was a beautiful part of the country.

Afternoon slid into evening; it wasn't now getting dark until well after eight o'clock. The unseasonably sultry air was threatening a thunder storm, but none came. So proud was I of my green fingered efforts, that I lingered outside long after dark, going indoors only to fetch a pullover or another cup of tea. Finally it was time to go to bed.

That night, I woke inexplicably, at around two in the morning. The warmth of the night was not abating and I was restless. Sleep had deserted me, leaving me listening to the rustle of the trees outside in the tender breeze. I got out of bed, wondering whether to potter downstairs and opened the curtains slightly to peer out. The night was black, the moon having set, and clouds were covering most of the stars. I hadn't switched a light on, and my eyes gradually adjusted to the dark. I began to perceive a shape below me in the garden, a white or grey misty haze by the gate which looked as if it was, again, open. Perhaps my eyes were clogged up with sleep. I peered yet more intensely, but couldn't work out if I was actually seeing anything at all. Was it just a trick of the poor light? A smear on the glass, or the reflection of my own body on the inside of the window pane? I moved slowly from side to side to give my eyes a different angle of view, but still I could not ascertain whether I was actually seeing anything or not. Then, all of a sudden, the misty shape seemed to take on a more solid appearance and it looked for a moment as if a face and a pair of dark eyes were peering up at me - not the face and eyes of an animal - but again, it wasn't discernible what I was actually seeing. Whatever it was, if anything, it had seemed to look right at me, but was I even visible in the dark window above? I couldn't be sure that I would be perceptible through a narrow gap between the dark curtains. The shape, or whatever it was, began to fade.

I threw on some jeans, a pullover and some trainers and grabbed my keys before heading downstairs. I didn't turn on any lights, but grabbed a torch from the cupboard by the back door, as I quietly went outside. Looking about revealed the garden to be exactly as I had left it, but just as I had thought, the gate was indeed open and I had definitely shut it before retiring. There was something whitish over by the gate, but it was too little and didn't look as if it would account for the shape I had witnessed from above. As I approached the small patch of whiteness, I switched on the torch, and discovered that it was a scrap of white gauze, the sort gardeners use to protect their plants from late frosts. It had clearly blown here on the breeze and got itself snagged on a low part of the hedging next to the gate. Kneeling to pick it up I glanced back up towards my bedroom window to try to figure whether this had been the source of my vision. Impossible to say from down here.

I stepped down onto the tracks. The breath of the wind was cool on my face. Glancing to my right, in the direction of the tunnel, and my previous night time walk, I again seemed to detect something white and misty in the distance. It was too faint to be anything definite, but once more something about it wouldn't let me ignore it as if it were a trick of the light, or a flurry of smoke on a gust of air. I began to pace slowly towards it down the line, my eyes transfixed on the shape ahead, which my senses deceived me at one moment was the shape and size of a deer, and at another moment was the shape and size of a person, and then at the next moment that it was nothing at all. I wasn't sure whether this apparition was constantly changing before me, or whether my own senses were being lulled by the dark, to see first one thing and then another.

I rounded the corner and saw the tunnel entrance looming before me as it had done on my previous walk. Just as dark and ominous, if not more so, on this moonless night. Something in-between the rails made me stop and bend down. As I picked it up I was amazed to recognise another tin, the same as the one that I had found in my loft, with an Edwardian girl on the lid, and tarnished in that same bronze colouring. What an incredible coincidence to find another, exactly identical tin! I prized open the lid to see what, if anything, would lay inside, and a momentary turn in my stomach began to prophesy exactly what I would find within. It was no idle prophecy, however, for as I had begun to fear only moments before hand, this was no coincidence, because this was not another tin. It was the same tin as the one that I had unearthed in my own attic. There, inside, was the folded piece of notepaper sheltering the the letters below. At least I was fairly certain that this was the same tin of letters; without taking each one out and reading them, there would be no way to tell.

My thoughts were abruptly interrupted by the familiar hum of the rails that indicated an approaching train. I didn't have time to contemplate the fact that this was half past two in the morning and that there were no trains due for hours. What did that matter anyway? The sound of the rails wasn't lying; there was undeniably a train approaching, and I was in the middle of the tracks. I desperately scanned forward and back to try to work out from which direction the train would be approaching, knowing all the time that I had but a few seconds to find this out, and decide which track to stand on; confusion, panic, anger at myself

- all steaming through my head: What would it feel like to be hit by a train? Next the lights of the approaching train, piercing the darkness of the tunnel in front of me.

Throwing myself leftwards, over the other track, I careered into the undergrowth as far away from both tracks as I could get. I didn't feel my arms grazing and legs getting scratched through my jeans on the dry, gritty ballast, and thought nothing of the wretched tin that I had found, dropping it onto the tracks as I dived out of harm's way. The roar of the train all but burst my eardrums, as if punishing me for my stupidity. There was a rush of noise and a turbulence of air as the train belted past. All at once, the scream of the engines was fading. A two-carriage multiple unit train, probably on an empty stock movement, but going apace, seemingly so much quicker than when I watched them benignly pass the end of the garden during the day. I was left lying on the trackside, my face in the stones, feeling ashamed and foolish. My left arm, bruised and most likely bleeding, now ached from where I had fallen on it.

I slowly picked myself up, half expecting to hear the train slow down in the distance, but its roar petered out, leaving me in the hope that I hadn't been seen by the driver. That thought hastened me back to my senses. If a person was reported to be on the line, I didn't want to be up and about, but safely tucked up in bed. There was the tin lying where I had dropped it in between the two rails, unharmed as the train had passed right over the top of it. Gathering it up, I hobbled back home to examine my wounds further in the light.

Placing the tin most deliberately on the floor just inside the back door, I went into the bathroom. Fortunately, my wounds, such as they were, were superficial. I washed them and they stung a bit, but it served me right for being such an idiot. Retribution indeed for a folly that had very nearly cost me far more.

Dismissing further thoughts of wispy white forms luring me from my slumber, I returned to bed, but slept fitfully, dreaming of the police arriving to question me about my whereabouts in the early hours, and asking if I had seen anyone trespassing on the tracks overnight.

CHAPTER 11

That disquieting feeling that I might be in trouble if the police came calling, was still with me when I woke up and lingered on and off all day. Luckily no one came to the door, and I began to hope that my adventure had gone unseen by the driver. After all I had worn dark clothes and should have been lying face down in the gravel as I came into view of the train driver. The tin sat resolutely by the back door, where I had left it. I thought no more about strange cloudy shapes, or at least I tried not to.

Around midday, I plucked up the courage to open the tin and examine its contents further. As far as I could tell, the contents were identical to the one I had found, and then re-placed, in the attic. The only thing to do then, was to get out the step ladder and see for myself. Verification gave me little satisfaction. There was no tin in the loft. I even went right up inside, although I was sure I'd left it within easy reach, and therefore perfectly in view, from the open hatch. It too had followed the keys, the watch, Ray's tape-measure, and Sarah's shoe out of the house of its own accord, only this time it had gone further, down onto the actual tracks and towards the tunnel. A new and unwelcome development. I certainly didn't want to wander down there every time I lost something. I made a mental note to always keep my wallet on my person from now on, sleeping with it beside my bed, even though this felt like the compulsive behaviour of a paranoiac. Small consolation was that I could now be almost certain that these odd disappearances were unlikely to be my own lapses of memory, or even some bizarre, extreme case of sleep walking. Asleep or not, I don't think I'd have got far walking down the tracks in bare feet, without waking up, or coming to some serious harm.

I felt no desire to go outside today, maybe because the weather, although still warm, was grey, overcast and quite humid, with a strong wind thrusting the trees about. I stayed indoors, cleaning the house, like a thing possessed, vacuuming corners of rooms and wiping parts of furniture that no one would ever see. I was glad of the diversion that the evening out at the theatre would provide and willed the clock anxiously towards six o'clock; dusting gratuitously; polishing furiously.

I was in the car at five to six keen to leave the house behind. The events of the previous night had not left me hating my new home: far from it. I still loved the solitude and the open skies and my lack of close neighbours. However, you can have too much of a good thing, and I was feeling confused and fractious, waiting for sufficient time to pass before I could assure myself that no policeman would be knocking at the door asking me my whereabouts at two o'clock the previous morning. It was a needless worry, but I've always been one to worry about hypotheticals, working myself into a state of angst. It was the same as a teacher, worrying that my students' results would be poor and that I'd be held to account and placed under competency proceedings. It never occurred, but I worried about it as if it were as certain as night following day. I was partly intrigued by my mystery - the prospect of solving what, or who, was moving things about for no apparent reason - and it fed a need within me for excitement. At the same time there was also a need to get away and view my problem from a distance, so as to gain a more reasonable perspective.

Sitting in a strange pub with Belinda and her friends did prove to be such a tonic. Imelda Staunton was there, and her real name turned out to be Gwen, but I had to make a conscious effort not to call her Imelda. Two other couples joined us for the pre-performance drinks: Vikki and Leonie, a couple who lived in Newstead, and Ian and Kate, from a village called Hollingford about ten miles away. The usual introductions about what everyone did for a living being over, the conversation turned to my new house and how I was settling in to my life in Poppington.

"I asked Mum about the train robbery," said Belinda. "She remembers it well, although she was only about ten years old at the time. It happened shortly before the Queen's Coronation and the events are all a bit confused in her mind, but she says that, while the whole country was focused on the new, young Queen, the locals were all less inclined to celebrate because it was a bit of a 'dark time'. In fact, she didn't say much more, as if even the mention of it stirred up a rather unpleasant feeling."

Ian asked where the information had come from and I told him about the book and the close proximity of my house to the tunnel where the event had taken place. Leonie described the entire affair as "thrilling", and Vikki dryly commented that nothing exciting like that had ever happened in Newstead since. Kate wondered how easy it would be to find a newspaper from back then to get some more details, especially about the culprit who had been so mercilessly executed for his crimes, and Belinda said she'd see what the library could uncover, though it might mean going to the main library in Elchester. Gwen said very little, but seemed to peer at me intensely, especially if she thought I wasn't looking. She seemed a little socially inept, and I found her silly stare and banal grin quite annoying. Clearly my new life in isolation was making me less tolerant of other people's foibles. (Although, then again maybe I have always been like that?)

The performance finished at about a quarter to ten. I wasn't sure I'd really understood it much, never having studied it at school. I couldn't quite make out if the sorcerer-guy was supposed to be good or evil. I wish I'd had the sense to read a synopsis of it beforehand to give me some clue as to what was going on, but no one seemed over impressed by the production, so my ignorance went unnoticed in the after-performance con-flab. Ian and Kate walked off towards the car park, Ian shaking my hand, "Nice to have met you" and Kate endorsing, "Yes you must join us again. Belinda can let you know when we next go out for a drink."

Leonie and Vikki linked hands and Vikki said, "Come on Gwen, we'll walk you home," and Gwen, rather reluctantly followed them.

Left alone with Belinda, I said, "Thanks again for inviting me along. It was so good to meet some people from around here. Most of my friends live in Elchester or Wilthorpe, and they're a bit too far away to just pop out for a quick drink."

"That's not a problem at all," she replied. "We usually go out on a Friday or a Saturday evening. You seem to get on well with everyone. I'll let you know next time we do something if you want."

"Yes please. I did get along with everyone, although Gwen's rather quiet."

"She's a funny character and maybe a little shy around new people. She'll be more talkative once she knows you better. But she's long been a friend of the family. In fact, it was Gwen who encouraged me to apply for the job at the library. You wouldn't think it to look at her, but she's a leading light in the local ramblers association." It was certainly true that I would never have pictured Gwen striding out across the hills with nothing but a cropped stick and a slab of Kendal mint cake.

"Oh, by the way," Belinda continued, "one place

you can go to find out more about the history of the railway is the pub near the station in the village. I believe they have quite a lot of old memorabilia up on the walls in there - or at least they used to - it's a while since I've been in. My Mum's not one for going to the pub, but I have a vague memory that there were a few old photos and things hanging up, as a kind of themed-pub type of thing. Usually I go for a drink here in town. There are several nice old pubs here."

"Do you live nearby?" I asked.

"Just round the corner, over there," she said, nodding across the car park. We meandered slowly in that general direction.

"My car's over that side too."

We said our goodbyes as we reached my car, and I stood and watched her go towards her house, one in a row of terraces in a street off the car park. I watched the lights turn on and then dim as she closed the curtains.

Then I too jumped into the car and made for home.

*

The following day, the urge to get away was still strong, since the apprehension caused by the close encounter with the train still hung about me, or about the house, I'm not sure which. I set off early for a nice long cycle ride before the weather got too hot, planning to lunch at *The Railway* pub on my way back home. The exercise and air cleansed me of my uneasiness, and the discovery of a new network of quiet country lanes beyond Goose Hill provided yet more picture-book scenes of English country charm. At one point, I found a footpath, suitable for a mountain bike, which took me through an orchard of blossoming fruit trees. After four hours, I was certainly ready for my pub lunch. In fact I was starving and almost regretted cycling so far. It was still early, and only just after midday, and although most of the other customers had opted for a seat in the beer garden, I was glad of the shelter from the sun that the coolness inside the pub provided. The appearance of the pub had been considerably brightened by the addition of some exquisite hanging baskets, festooning the frontage, and certainly giving the impression that summer was well on its way. I ordered the roast chicken dinner, glad that it was only a fifteen minute ride to home.

My order made at the bar, I freshened myself up in the toilets before settling myself down at a table. Belinda had been right, and the pub had indeed themed itself to a large extent around the historic railway theme. Above me was a picture of Poppington Station, taken in 1910, and a further examination of the photos on the wall revealed more views of the local railway and the pub itself through the ages. What I wasn't expecting, and what really interested me, was the great play that the pub was obviously making of its connection to the *Great Train Robbery of 1953*. It seemed that the Robert Wallace, mentioned in the library book as the murderous local who robbed and killed the diamond courier on his way to Belgium, was none other than a previous landlord of this very pub. Kudos indeed for the current owners to cash in on.

Three pictures immediately caught my eye. One was of Robert Wallace himself, photographed shortly after his arrest, his eyes staring defiantly at the camera whilst handcuffed to a police officer. Another was of the unfortunate train, taken at Poppington Station the morning following the incident, and presumably held there whilst the line was closed and the investigation was underway. According to the caption, the train service, which connected with a boat to Antwerp at Salthaven, had the romantic name *The Diamond Belle.* The third was of an old hollow tree, somewhere near Poppington, where Wallace had hidden out during the two weeks that he was "on the run". The caption did not reveal why he had stayed in the local area instead of making off with his booty.

Several newspaper accounts were also in picture frames on the wall. One dated 25th May 1953 detailed the crime and the police hunt for the criminal, or criminals, involved. A second, dated 10th June, recorded the capture of Wallace, stories of his hideout in the old tree, and praising Inspector Clegg, who had led the investigation and man-hunt to its satisfactory conclusion. One further article, from the beginning of September, reported the results of the trial at Salthaven Assizes, the judge's sentencing, and Wallace's refusal to betray where he had stashed the diamonds, knowledge of which the newspaper speculated he was wanting to bargain for clemency from the gallows. When asked about the hiding place of the diamonds, Wallace merely said cryptically, "*No one will ever know where that flower now blooms,*" and otherwise remained silent. No such deal was made, according to a fourth report, and Wallace was duly executed in October, at Gurney Prison just outside Elchester.

Engrossed in these artefacts meant that I was well and truly occupied whilst waiting for my meal. Despite it being rather a hot day for a roast, I attacked it ravenously and ordered a coffee afterwards. It wasn't the best roast dinner I had ever had, but nor was it, by any means, the worst, and I was grateful not to have to wash up afterwards. I lingered for a while over my coffee under the shade of a tree, reluctant to get back on the bike again even for such a short distance. Before setting off home, I made one last trip inside to re-examine details of the Poppington Train Robbery on the walls indoors.

CHAPTER 12

On Tuesday, I finally dragged myself in the car to a retail park on the outskirts of Wilthorpe to order a new kitchen and bathroom, which appeared as if they were going to take up to a month to arrive. The weather had remained warm and sunny, and the thermometer climbed a little higher each day, along with a pressing humidity, making sleep difficult. One disadvantage of my new life in the country was the number of mosquitos that flew in through the open window, keeping me awake with their high pitched whine as they dived at my ears. Sleeping with the window closed was out of the question, such was the heat, and I shed the duvet for a mere sheet to sleep beneath.

Nothing else disappeared from the house, apparating again on the steps by the gate. Even the gate itself behaved by staying shut. I had no further appetite for any more midnight walks along the railway line.

Wednesday night slipped into Thursday

morning, and the bedside clock resolutely shone the minutes past one o'clock and then two o'clock. These late nights, and the inability to sleep in the stifling heat, meant that I was at least waking later and later each morning, sleeping more comfortably as the room grew cooler. Tonight, however, was particularly bad. Turning the light on in my bedroom would have been to invite every biting insect through the open window to dine on me. So it was downstairs that I repaired, drinking water and trying to concentrate on reading more of *Twenty Thousand Leagues Under The Sea.* I sat, brooding in the armchair, in the clammy heat.

After twenty minutes of reading the same page over and over, it was time to give up, and I switched the light off and wandered into the kitchen. As my eyes got used to the dark, I gazed out of the back door letting the night air cool me down. A few stars twinkled in between the clouds and a pair of bats swooped about gorging on insects. The plants of the garden stood out as stark shadows against the gloomy sky, the awkward untrimmed shape of the hedge screening the railway, swaying in the fluffy air.

At last, I decided to retire back upstairs. When I was about half way across the kitchen, I thought I heard a noise from overhead; a creaking sound from the ceiling of the middle room. I stopped and stood perfectly still in the kitchen doorway, listening intently. The noise came again, very distinctly like a low thud from the floorboards in the room above. It repeated itself again, and again, about ten times, like slow footsteps pacing across the room above me. I stared up at the ceiling, straining my ears for any tell-tale sounds that might indicate what it was. The final thud was much fainter, as if, walking across the room, the footsteps had finally reached the doorway and stopped on the tiny landing at the top of the stairs between the two bedrooms.

The silence that followed was so empty that my ears found it difficult to focus. Had I really heard footsteps from the room above, or was it just the natural creak of the floorboards slowly contracting after the heat of the day? Had opening and closing the back door caused some flow of air through the house to make such a sound? Standing motionless, barely breathing, I waited, as the clock on the wall slowly ticked away the seconds, one, two, three, four, five...

Next, unmistakably, came the soft squeaky groan of the door to the front bedroom. Someone, or something, was upstairs. A sudden gust of wind angered the trees and a bird screeched nearby. I felt, in that dark space, a shuddering sense of my own solitude, my vulnerability in this empty old house, miles from the nearest neighbour. I considered running outside, but realised there was nowhere to go. (At night we can all feel lost). This thought pulled me to my senses slightly. Perhaps I had imagined the noises. Maybe I had an intruder. It didn't seem possible that a burglar could be upstairs. True, all the windows had been open, but how could anyone have gotten in undetected? After all, I had been up, sleepless, all night, completely awake and in full hearing of anyone entering the house. It just did not seem possible that anyone could have got in by the front or back doors whilst I had been upstairs trying to get to sleep. Getting in through the windows would have created enough racket to have alerted me. I walked through to the front door checking it was shut and locked, before returning to the bottom of the stairs.

"Hello!" I called up, my voice echoing up the stair well. Nothing: except the ticking of the clock. No more creaking door. No further footsteps. Only then did it occur to me to switch on the light, wondering why on earth I hadn't thought of doing this before. It was as if the unexplained sounds and the bewitching darkness had paralysed my common sense. I felt for the switch on the left hand wall at the bottom of the stairs, it clicked and in a moment the light flashed on and then off, with a barely audible ping; the bulb picking a most inopportune moment to blow. I returned to the cupboard by the back door for the torch, grabbed it and noticed that the tin of letters was no longer there on the floor, where I was sure I had left it since that night I had retrieved it from the railway line. I'd not quite known what to do with it, since hiding it in the loft had not prevented it reappearing outside. At least here by the door I could keep an eye on it. Surely it had been there, by my feet, only a few minutes ago? Or had it? I honestly couldn't remember.

Flicking on the torch, I took a deep breath, and strode purposefully back to the stairs. Fortune favours the brave, so I went straight up. As I was mounting the last few, I stopped abruptly to listen. Feeling a chill, for the first time that night, I wondered which door I should try first. The door to the right which led to my bedroom and from where the sound of the footsteps had seemed to come? Or the door to the left, into the front spare room, which I was sure I had heard squeak just moments ago? Both doors stood slightly ajar but not open wide enough to see in. Standing on the small square landing, I pushed open the left door - the door to the front bedroom - flinching at its tell-tale squeal, despite knowing that this time I was the cause of the noise. I could make out the dark shapes of the wardrobe, the bed and the chest of drawers. Every thing was still and silent. It almost felt too still. The persistent noise of the trees, swaying outside in the breeze, had suddenly ceased. Where was the ticking of the clock? It was as if the whole universe had suddenly stopped; halted, waiting. I was holding my breath, unwilling to breathe out, to even make the slightest noise. Then there, by the window, I sensed, in the periphery of the torch beam, a dark motionless figure, half-silhouetted against the night sky, the other half, hidden beside the hanging curtains. All at once I thrust the torch light in the direction of the profile, and with my left hand slapped the light switch, in a flash of fear, wanting to end this awful terror and see *it* finally, whatever it was, once and for all.

The light went on, extinguishing the torch beam with immediate effect, and my eyes blinked in the sudden change from the dark. At least this bulb stayed on. And there, where I had seen the shape, the figure half-visible against the window, I saw nothing at all. No person, no shadow, not even the curtain swaying in the draught of the open window.

I realised I was trembling, and the trembling turned to shivering, and, as I slowly digested what I had seen, or thought I had seen, I felt nauseous. Relief from a scare, no doubt, but maybe also disgust at being so alarmed by the antics of my own over-active imagination. Such foolishness, to be daunted in such a way, in my own home; by creaking floorboards, doors squeaking in the draught and fanciful dark shadows. I regained my natural breathing, and I must have stood there recovering in that front room for about three, or maybe four, minutes.

Finally. Finally, it was time for bed. I was tired and cold and I wanted, more than anything else, to be cuddled up and cosy under the sheets, or better still, the duvet itself. I switched off the light and turned round to go into my own bedroom, closing the squeaky door firmly behind me.

As I switched on the light in my own room, I saw it. The tin: the tin full of letters, with that precocious Edwardian picture on the lid. There it was, on my pillow.

CHAPTER 13

The next morning I awoke at half past nine, and the sun was already bearing down its heat, in what was preparing to be an even hotter, muggier day than yesterday. Of course the first thing I saw on waking was that wretched tin, lying on the floor where I had despondently thrown it the previous night. This reminded me of my fright, the momentary relief from that fear as I realised that I had seen and heard nothing, and then my subsequent despair on discovering that I had been duped more in my relief than in my fright. The angels that had lulled away those horrors during my sleep were scattered to the winds. Now they were replaced by dark memories stirred up like a heavy sediment. I sat on the edge of the bed, rubbing the rough stubble on my chin, wondering what this day would bring.

Thinking about everything was getting me nowhere. It didn't matter whether I was laying in bed, sitting downstairs or pottering in the garden:

contemplating all these mysteries was driving me mad. I just couldn't sort it out in my mind and the more I considered everything, the more confused I became.

I decided to look at things from an alternative perspective. Firstly, whatever was going on, I was still happy in the new house. I knew this because the minute I asked myself if I regretted leaving my old place, in Avenue Green, the answer was a definite *no*. Secondly, I knew that leaving work last Christmas had been the best decision I had made in a long time, and that the kind of worry I was experiencing at the moment was infinitely less tedious than the stresses of a teaching job. True, I had considered going on a world trip after I finished work, but seeing *Railway Cottage* on the market and buying the place had put that idea on hold indefinitely. Something about travelling the world seemed a bit like running away, until I could come up with a place I really wanted to visit. The Middle East was always high on my list, but just lately that had been ruled out by a political unrest, which threatened to flood the region. My new house had been a welcome project.

So I was happy, with no regrets, and the fact that I couldn't solve the problem of the gate, the tin and the moving objects was merely, I decided, a practical diversion. Maybe, however, I should give further thought to doing some voluntary work, to make my life less self-centred and more focused on others.

Thinking of the tin again, however, reminded me of Sarah's shoe and that we had tentatively agreed to meet up again this coming weekend. I wondered if I would benefit from a visit to hers, to get away from the house, but that sounded too negative. Perhaps if I told her about what had happened she would want to revisit. I would phone and let her make the decision.

Which is why, on the next day (Friday), I found myself listening for her car at about half past six. Naturally she had been happy for me to go to her, but when she heard about the tin and the footsteps upstairs, she said there was no contest.

"That settles it then," she had said. "I've always wanted to investigate a haunted house and I've got a few things I'll be bringing with me!"

"Like what?" I'd asked.

"You'll see," came the reply. And with that she had laughed and rung off.

Whilst we ate a hastily prepared salad in the garden, Sarah admired all my horticultural efforts and quizzed me further about my adventure on the railway line with the wispy white apparition, and finding the tin. I'd brought the tin back downstairs and as we ate, she carefully went through the letters one by one reading some of them aloud, interjected with her comments about what she thought they were.

"Definitely written by a bloke," was one such comment. "I bet he was writing to her about meeting up," was another. "I reckon she was married," and, "I wonder when these were written?" She wanted me to describe in detail again about what the wispy shape in the garden had looked like, and to show her exactly where it had been. Then she wanted to know all about the footsteps, and the silhouette by the window in the upstairs front bedroom. ("How exciting! That's where I'll be sleeping!"), and as we'd finished eating, we went in and she stood downstairs in the kitchen doorway, whilst I went up and tried to replicate the sounds that I had heard by stomping across the bedroom floor, first in barefoot, then in shoes. Sarah was thorough, and keen to investigate, but, as she said more than once, still quite sceptical.

"I could certainly hear you as you walked across the room," she said. "Here, let me try," and off she went to give me the benefit of what she had heard from the room below. "Was that like what you heard?" she asked, on returning back down. Without waiting for an answer, she opened her bag and began to pull out various items. A wooden cross, a card game and a small black electrical device, about the size of a TV remote control.

"This cross was bought in Jerusalem," she explained, "and is made of wood from an olive tree. We'll place it on a piece of paper, draw round it, and leave it as a trigger object, to see if it moves. These cards we'll make into a ouija board and see if we can contact any spirits." She beamed. "This is so exciting! And this," she waved the small black object, "is an EMF meter, which measures the electro-magnetic field. Wherever we feel there's any paranormal activity we point this and see if the dial moves to indicate a *presence*. And also..." she rummaged again in her bag, "... this is an electronic thermometer, to investigate any changes in temperature: It's supposed to get colder when there's paranormal activity." All her ghost-hunting items placed proudly on the table, Sarah stood smiling, like a child displaying her toys, waiting expectantly to see what I would say.

"Where did you get all this?" I asked.

"I used to be really into *Most Haunted*," she replied, as if that answered my question.

"Does any of it work? I didn't know you had any of this stuff."

"Well, that I can't tell you. I've never had an opportunity to use any of it. When I got your call last night, I went rummaging through all my cupboards looking for it all. I can't wait to try everything out."

"Crosses from The Holy Land, electro-whatsit readers, ouija boards... Sarah, you never fail to amaze me!"

"Now where shall we set all this up?" she asked herself, gazing round the room, arms on her hips.

"Dessert first!" I cried, going into the kitchen. "Let's eat this in the garden."

Sarah swallowed her strawberries and ice cream before I'd even got half way through mine, and not waiting for me to finish, she was up and into the house again. When I walked in she was busy in the downstairs front room. The card game was a kind of scrabble-type thing, with cards instead of tiles, called *Lexicon*. The cards were being arranged alphabetically around the coffee table, alongside two hand-made cards, one reading *Yes*, the other reading *No*. In the centre stood an upturned glass.

"Do you have a piece of clean paper, preferably plain A4?" she asked, without looking up. I went upstairs obediently. When I returned, the ouija board was complete, and Sarah took the piece of paper from me, carefully drawing round the small wooden cross with a pencil and clearing a space on the dining table in the back room upon which to place it. Anxious to be of some use I set about moving my odds and ends away and clearing more space. "Do you have any candles?"

"It's not even dark yet."

I fetched some from the kitchen nonetheless.

"Yes we will have to wait until nightfall," Sarah called after me, "but we want to get set up first. Nights are short this time of the year, so we won't have long." She took the candles from me, placing them either side of the trigger object. "I'm just wondering if we ought to place this upstairs," she continued. "That's where a lot of the activity has been happening."

"*Supposed* activity," I corrected her. Sarah's scepticism seemed to have waned somewhat.

She took the cross and its piece of paper upstairs, and returned saying, "I've left it on the floor in the front bedroom, by the window where you said you saw the figure outlined against the window..."

"... Or *thought* I did."

"...Neither of us are to go in there unaccompanied, so that we can verify that *if* it moves it wasn't the other person playing tricks."

I grinned. "I wouldn't do that to you."

"Yes you would. I remember when you sent that letter to everyone on the staff, telling them that tomorrow was going to be a holiday. It was on official school notepaper and everything."

"And they never found out who did it," I laughed.

"The Headmaster thought it was Andy Bruce,

the Head of Science!" Sarah laughed as well. "Ah! We had some fun in those days didn't we? But," and she wagged her finger at me in mock disapproval, "It *does* mean that I *do* know what you're capable of!" She laid the EMF meter and the thermometer on the table next to the candles. "Right then, I think there's a bottle of wine in the garden that needs finishing; just what I need to psyche myself up for tonight."

And it was funny how sitting there in the garden, drinking that wine, I did actually feel the excitement rising as the darkness fell. We gradually fell more and more silent, mellowed by the alcohol, or quiet in anticipation, I couldn't quite tell: probably a bit of both. I was just waiting for Sarah to give the go-ahead.

As the sun set just after nine we went indoors. Sarah lit the candles and we both went upstairs to check the trigger object. The cross was firmly within its outline on the piece of paper on the floor by the window. We then took the EMF meter around the house, Sarah pointing it with a steady hand in various areas where I had reported "activity". It naturally registered each time it went near an AC electrical source and most electrical appliances made it light up, emit a beeping noise and move the dial. It only seemed to react unusually in my bedroom, over near the window, but I resisted saying that this could have been electric cables under the floorboards, not wanting to rain on Sarah's parade.

Finally, Sarah said it was dark enough to try the ouija board and we sat ourselves either side of the coffee table in the front room, curtains drawn, candles lit, our fingers placed on the upturned glass.

"If there are any spirits with us in the room tonight, we welcome them," Sarah began. "We come to speak to you in peaceful terms and ask that you communicate with us using the letters on this board." She paused. "Is there anyone in the room with us?" Another long silent pause. Nothing happened. The glass remained still and there were no noises. "Is there anyone with us here tonight?... Is anyone there?... We wish you no harm... Please, if there is anyone here move this glass on the table."

Silence. "Is there anyone here with us in this room?"

Nothing.

Sarah continued; "Please send us a sign, if you are here with us..."

I sniggered. "Shhh! They won't communicate if they think you're laughing at them..." she reprimanded. "Is there anyone here with us in this room tonight?..."

We sat silently, the candlelight casting weird shadows across the room. This must have continued for another ten minutes, with Sarah continuing to evoke the activity of the spirit world, myself sitting finger on glass, and the candle flickering, but all to no avail. Eventually she said, "Let's have a break."

We went into the kitchen, and I opened another bottle of wine.

"What next?" I asked.

"We'll go around the house with the EMF meter and the electronic thermometer, and check the trigger object. Then we'll try the ouija board again."

We spent the next hour doing all of these things, but disappointingly had no results. Even the EMF meter failed to perform in the back bedroom, and by the end I thought the whole thing had been a harmless waste of time. Sarah was less despondent and said not to worry, as there was always tomorrow night.

*

Indeed there was. We had spent the day sitting in the garden and lunching in Newstead. Sarah had ventured again into the bag shop, but this time bought nothing. The day had been humid and cloudy and as evening drew closer it began to threaten rain. A strong, warm wind started to blow in from the south-west.

We had retreated into the front room with our glasses of wine at about eight o'clock and were sitting pondering the ouija board. Sarah had been busy on her phone researching uses of the board on the Internet.

"We've got to touch the board with our hands first," she instructed. "The board is known as a planchette and it can take up to fifteen minutes for the spirits to communicate. *Only people who are serious and respectful should use the board. Do not treat it as if it were a game,*" she read, giving me a look. "*Do not use the board under the influence of alcohol...* Oh well, never mind... *If the planchette starts to spell out disturbing or frightening messages, end the session immediately.*"

There was a loud knock at the door and we both jumped. I opened it to find Belinda standing on the doorstep.

"Hello," I said.

"Hi," she answered before I could have a chance to say anything more. "I'm off out for a drink at *The Ship* with Ian, Kate, Leonie and Vikki, and I was just driving past on the way back from Mum's. I thought I'd drop by and see if you wanted to join us."

"Oh I'm sorry, I'm busy this evening," I replied, hoping the disappointment showed in my voice. The thought of another fruitless seance with Sarah was not quite as appealing as a trip to the pub with Belinda. "Won't you come in?"

"I won't if that's ok as I'll be late for meeting the others," she answered. I opened the door further in an attempt to show Sarah sitting behind me - that I had a genuine reason for not going out and that I was not just fobbing her off.

"I've got a friend down to visit," I said. "This is Sarah, an old friend, who's dropped by to see the place." I opened the door wider, but not wide enough, I hoped, that Belinda could see the stupid ouija board.

"Hi," said Sarah looking up.

"Hello."

Awkward.

"Well I'm sorry if I disturbed you."

"... No not at all..." I tried to interject.

"I'd better get going. I should have texted. Sorry." She looked embarrassed. "Bye."

"Thanks anyway," I called after her, trying not to sound pathetic, but failing completely, as she jumped into the car and started up the engine.

I closed the door.

"Well now I feel like a complete gooseberry," said Sarah as I sat down heavily on the armchair.

"What d'you mean?" I remonstrated, "I've only met her about four times. There's nothing going on."

"I didn't mean you, Dumbo, I meant her."

"How d'you make that out? You hardly spoke to her."

"It's nothing to do with that. She looked at me with daggers."

"She did not."

"It's a woman thing. And I can tell by the way you're jiggling your foot that you like her too."

"You think she likes me?" I said, ignoring her teasing.

"Men! Why are you always so blind to these things?" Then she said with a cheeky smile, "you can always go after her you know! I can make myself scarce."

"No, I don't want to seem too desperate..." (I had actually already considered it).

As if reading my mind, Sarah said; "Keep her dangling. Let her think she's got a rival - she'll be all the keener for it - not that she should worry. After all, I am an *old* friend."

"Now *you're* talking like a bloke."

"You're right. What do I know? My success in that department hardly qualifies me to give advice. Anyway, she's nice: Tall, slim, long dark hair... the bitch! I hate her!" she joked.

"You really think someone like her would look twice at me?"

"Don't run yourself down." Sarah always had the knack of saying the right thing.

"Look are you sure this ouija board rubbish really works?" I asked walking through to the kitchen.

"I've no idea, but we'll give it one more try later, once it gets dark."

Thick heavy raindrops were beginning to fall against the kitchen window, and I could almost feel the garden heaving a sigh of relief to be quenched at last. Mesmerised by the long-awaited rain, we stood looking out of the window waiting for nightfall. I put on some music and we opened another bottle of wine.

Eventually the clock got round to ten and we decided that it was time enough. Sarah began with the usual exhortations just like the previous evening, and we both sat, fingers poised on the glass waiting for something to happen.

"Is there anyone in the house with us tonight who would like to speak to us... we come peacefully and we wish you no harm... we want you to communicate with us using this board... If there is anyone here, please move the glass... please move the glass towards the *Yes* position..." We sat in silence. The glass did not move. Then, upstairs we heard the front bedroom door creak. We both held our breath straining for further noises. Nothing. Once again the ticking of the clock and the weather outside were the only things we could hear.

Sarah began again: "Was that you creaking the door upstairs...? If it was, do it again..." No response. "We heard the door upstairs creak and we ask if there is anyone here with us in this house tonight?"

"Probably just the wind," I conjectured.

"Shhh!" I was admonished. "We want to ask you about the gate opening by itself. Was that you...?" Silence. "We want to ask you about the things that have gone missing and ended up by the gate or on the railway line, like Ed's watch, or my shoe. Was that you?" We paused and listened. "What about the tin full of letters? Are they yours?" Immediately the door upstairs slammed shut. We both gasped. Sarah looked at me her eyes narrowed. I did not say a thing, but was wondering whether this was a communication for real, or just a draught through the upstairs rooms, causing the door to swing open and shut. We waited a while longer.

"Thank you for slamming the door... We want to know more about the letters... Were they written *by* you...? Were they written *to* you...? Please move the glass to answer the questions that we ask you..." The glass remained static. Sarah whispered after a while, as if to show she was now addressing me and not the spirits, "What about the trigger object? Lets go up and check it."

Dutifully I followed her up the stairs. "It's moved!" She exclaimed on entering her room. We both looked down at the cross sitting just outside its outline on the piece of paper.

"We never checked it before we began this evening," I said, aware that I was pouring a dampener on this potentially unexplainable event. "It could have shifted slightly as you've been coming in and out of the room during the day."

Sarah pondered. "You could be right. But then again, I think I'd have noticed if it'd moved when I came in earlier. I kept looking at it throughout the day. Of course, I didn't expect it to move during the day, because ghostly activity only usually happens at night," she said.

"Yes, why *is* that?" I asked, not without a tinge of irony.

Ignoring me, Sarah put the cross back within its outline and went round the room with the EMF meter. It bleeped a couple of times as it passed over the olive cross. Then we went back downstairs to the front room to continue our seance.

"Look!" Sarah said, entering the front room.

"What?"

"The glass! It's moved!"

The glass, which had been beneath our fingers in the centre of the coffee table was now standing, still upside down next to the letter T.

"What shall we do?" asked Sarah, although how she thought I could answer that, I do not know.

"Let's put it back in the middle," I suggested. This we did. We sat down and placed our fingers once more on the upturned glass. Sarah began her questioning again using similar questions to before, throwing in a few new ones about the trigger object for good measure. Each time the glass sat motionless.

Twenty or so minutes must have passed and we yielded no new results. I had already begun to suppose that one of us must have moved the glass subconsciously as we got up to go and see the trigger object and that we couldn't remember doing it. I didn't voice this opinion, however, but I did suggest a tea break in the kitchen, to which Sarah readily agreed.

It was nearly eleven o'clock by the time we had finished our brew, and I was beginning to feel slightly grizzly. Perhaps I had had too much wine, or maybe I was regretting not being able to go out with Belinda. Either way, I was getting tired and I always get irritable when I need my sleep. So I was poised to suggest going to bed as Sarah and I returned to the front room.

U.

The glass on the table had moved again. This time it was by the U. Or was it the T again, just a little out of position? The letters, of course were arranged around the table in alphabetical order.

"It's moved again!" Sarah was so excited, and I forgot all about my early night and became intrigued.

"Are you sure we put it back in the middle?" I asked, even though I knew we had.

"You know we did. Here let's do it again. We'll put it back in the middle and leave the room, and see where it moves next time. Will it go back to the T? What if its trying to spell something?"

"Is it the T? Or is it the U?" I asked

"Who knows, but we'll see what happens next." Sarah placed the glass back into the centre of the table and we both went back out of the room and into the kitchen. "How long should we stay out here? We were about ten minutes last time."

"Who knows how long it takes for the glass to move?"

"Damn," said Sarah. "I should've left my phone

in there recording what happens."

"You mean sounds?"

"Yes, and pictures. There's a video camera function on it."

Impatiently, we waited for about ten minutes, before venturing back into the front room. The upturned glass remained firmly in the middle of the ouija board, where we had left it. We deserted the room twice more in the hope that the glass would move again, but the spirits had stopped playing, or they'd performed enough for us for one night. My tiredness returned, and as it was nearing midnight, I suggested bed. Reluctantly Sarah agreed, but not without playing with the EMF meter again and a further check on the trigger object.

CHAPTER 14

I awoke with a start in the middle of the night. I remember being conscious that it was still dark outside, but did not immediately look towards the clock. Certain I had heard a noise, and that it was the noise that had awoken me, I listened again but could only hear the rain smacking on the window. Then I heard it again. A yell, or a scream, or a moan; I couldn't quite tell, but it sounded like Sarah, and it was coming from her bedroom. As I began to get quictly out of bed, I heard her call again, definitely a yell this time and much louder, and I forgot all about being cautious, rushed out of the room and opened her door.

As I went in, I found Sarah sitting up in bed, with the duvet pulled protectively around her, staring across the room in the direction of the built-in cupboard. The cupboard door was open and inside were all my old boxes, still unpacked and unsorted.

"I saw it!" she said. "Oh, Ed, I was so

frightened! I saw it. I saw it!"

"Saw what?"

"A figure, a person, a shape... I don't know, but I could swear there was someone there in that cupboard doorway."

I hastily walked over to the cupboard.

"There's no one here," I said. "Were you awake or were you dreaming?"

"I'm sure I was awake, but... I know that's what everyone says." Clearly confused, Sarah still sat in bed, a frozen look upon her face, staring at the void that was the cupboard doorway.

"Was the cupboard door closed when you went to bed?"

"Yes it was. I'm sure it was." She paused before continuing, "I know it sounds corny, but I felt a presence. I felt I was being watched, and it wasn't a nice feeling. It felt quite malevolent, quite evil."

I picked up the EMF meter and pointed it at the cupboard, keen to placate Sarah by returning to the fun of our earlier investigation. It made no noise. "Well maybe you *did* see something," I said. "Remember, I thought that I did. But it could also be a trick of the mind. That ouija board business earlier could have suggested all sorts to your imagination."

Sarah sat despondently, nodding, but saying nothing, still peering out from underneath the comfort of the duvet. "Are you gonna be ok in here?" I asked.

"What time is it?"

I wandered back to my bedroom to look at the clock radio, taking the opportunity to put on a robe. "It's three thirty-five," I said, returning. "I'm going down for a cuppa. You wanna join me?"

She nodded her assent with a shiver, and I handed her a fleece to put on over her pyjamas.

*

We were up late the following morning. Sarah and I had swapped beds after last night's incident, but I don't think either of us had got much sleep. I had been conscious of what Sarah had claimed to see over by the cupboard door, even though no further visions appeared. When sleep had come it had been fitful and, asleep or awake, I had that knotted feeling in my stomach such as I used to get the night before an exam.

It was Sunday and I knew Sarah would be leaving at some point. An unspoken, and somewhat awkward, ambivalence hung in the air. I felt as if I wanted her to go, so as to put all this ghost investigation nonsense to rest, yet on the other hand felt uneasy about being left alone again. Sarah was good company, but we both felt listless now. She too seemed in two minds about everything. I felt she wanted to go, but that she didn't want to appear to be abandoning me, or running away from her scare in the night. Usually, on a Sunday we would have gone for a walk, cooked a nice meal, and said our goodbyes in the afternoon, but there was a sense that neither of us had the appetite for that now. The weather seemed to match our mood. It was cold, and still raining. We both sat in the back room sipping our tea, staring aimlessly at the raindrops which slid unenthusiastically down the window pane.

Outside, everything had already taken on a much lusher, greener hue which, exacerbated by the grey clouds and heavy drizzle, enclosed the house in its cocoon of ageing hedgerows and trees, adding to the feeling of claustrophobia.

"I think I need to go for a walk," I said, trying to pull us out of our languor. The rain did not put me off. In fact, I almost felt I would enjoy feeling the rain on my face after such a long dry spell. I predicted it would also force Sarah into a decision about whether to stay or go, and sure enough, she replied;

"Do you mind if I head off now? I don't fancy a walk, and I'm feeling a little bit shame-faced about my fright last night. I reckon you were right and all that messing about with the ouija board made me have a nightmare. I'm sorry I woke you and made you rush in. I feel like such an idiot. But I think I'd rather get home early whilst there's no traffic and perhaps catch up on some sleep this afternoon. I'm sorry, Ed, you don't think I'm running away do you?"

She needed reassuring, and I was glad she had made a decision and that we weren't going to spend the rest of the day looking at each other awkwardly and twiddling our thumbs.

"I think you're right. Whether you saw something last night or dreamt it, makes little difference to how you feel today, because like the stuff that's happened to me, you just don't know what to make of it. I need to think things through. We both do. We definitely did not imagine that glass moving last night, so who knows what's going on? Why don't I ring you in the week, when we've both had time to think about it and we'll decide what, if anything, to do next?"

Smiling gratefully, Sarah got up and gave me a hug. "You gonna be all right here on your own?"

"I'll be fine, and if I get too spooked I'll jump in the car and come over to stay at yours!"

"Yes, you do that," she replied. "You know where I keep the spare key, if I'm out don't you?"

"Behind the water butt!" I said.

Sarah gathered her things together and was standing at the bottom of the stairs, bag in hand, within five minutes. I stood at the front door as she got into the car, and watched her smile and wave as she backed into the lane and drove away. Long after it was out of sight I remained standing there as the sound of her car finally, definitely, faded away, dissolving into the damp morning air; transfixed by the quiet chatter of raindrops in the newly formed puddles, pondering the act of turning around again, and closing my own front door.

I hadn't said anything to Sarah, but as we'd passed through the front room, I'd noticed that the glass on the coffee table was standing next to the letter N.

CHAPTER 15

The walk I took that day was probably one of the longest I have ever been on. Sarah must have left at about a quarter to twelve. I'd donned a rain coat, grabbed my keys, a bottle of water and a small packet of biscuits and was on my way as soon as I could get out of the front door. My stride was brisk and my mood was impetuous. Going up towards the Poppington Road, I remembered a footpath striking off towards the west, which I had not yet explored, and took this route, not caring that I didn't have a map and that I had no idea where I was going. The rain pitter-pattered onto my coat like tiny fingers: definitely the end of the good weather, I thought. On reaching the brow of the hill, the wind hounded the raindrops horizontally on a collision course with my face, but their wild valour simply urged me into their path. Onward I paced, further and further from the house, across the fields towards a grey curtain of woodland in the distance. I thought back to those recent hot sunny days, and previous walks and cycle rides when the countryside was like a giant yellow bowl, with sticky black roads diving deep between the hills, while white cottages basked in the heart of it. I remembered the objects that had disappeared, only to reappear at the gate, the chalky crosses on my bedroom floor, the garden I had cleared, Belinda dropping by with my wallet, the ghostly shape that had led me onto the railway line, the ouija board; so many things whirring about in my head, it was an effort to sort them all out and make any sort of sense. My hatred of my job - had it really been that bad after all? Certainly my dull house in suburbia had been. And from these perplexing pictures I returned to the jumbled present - the thick dull clouds, the lowering sky, the sharp wind and wet clothes.

My route led directly into the dripping trees. Inside the wood, a silence settled eerily - so complete that I might have been the only living soul on the planet. Trudging onwards, trying to maintain a steady westward direction, I must have gone wrong, for the pathway began to vanish, until eventually I was left standing in a small gap between the trees, where the ground was edged with the rusty leaves of last autumn. The morose grey clouds peered down, mocking me for a moment in this drizzly place, with the tortuous riddles of the past few days; chiding me from the gap in the tree-tops for fleeing my ghosts and goading me to venture deeper into this hostile woodland and chance my reaching the other side. I looked around me, wondering which way to go next, and foolishly forgot to take note of the direction from whence I had come, until I had little notion of whether I was proceeding forward or re-tracing my steps.

Striving onwards, the wet branches of the trees began to encroach on my face, stinging me as they pinged back and forth, whilst I tried to clear an avenue through them. Muttering profanities beneath my breath, I stumbled first this way, and then that way, eager to find a way through. Twice I nearly twisted my ankle as my foot dived into some treacherous hole concealed by rotting leaves, and I stubbed my toe time and again on some oblivious, forgotten tree root, dispiriting my mood further. Sliding on the wet leaves, I crawled through an area of coppice, almost bent double, as I shielded my eyes from the vicious twigs, getting no respite, when, on pushing in and out of one thicket, I merely ended up in another. After about fifteen minutes of this, shoving myself through one last time, I sat down on the dank ground.

Not knowing whether to laugh or cry, I picked myself up, cajoling myself into a more positive mood, trying to decide what to do next. The rain also picked this moment to get heavier and the pale clouds blackened in despair. I surveyed the route I had taken through the dense coppice, concluding that forward was better than back. Making a decision, I clambered through the next couple of trees and found myself in a less dense area. There seemed to be a way forward off to my left, though there was definitely no path. The ground began to slope downwards and the going became less difficult. Having lost all sense of direction long ago, I hoped that, as I had ascended *towards* the woodland, this descent would bring me out again. The air was still cold, and my sojourn on the ground had left me feeling chilly. I took deep breaths inhaling the smell of the damp woodland, treading ever downward between tree after tree.

I halted suddenly, smelling smoke. This was not the smell of cigarette smoke. This was a smell like a bonfire; noticeably clammy, of wet leaves, burning reluctantly and heavily, giving off mild but thick smokey puffs. I tried to figure out the direction from which these wafts were coming and as I stood, I heard the faint crackle a fire gives, coming from somewhere ahead, but slightly to the right.

Walking on, as softly as the leaves would allow, I began to make out a small camp-fire between the trees. There it was, there was no mistake about it. Not a wild fire, it was far too damp for that. A few days previously I would have assumed that in the tinder-dry conditions a small piece of abandoned glass could easily have started off a fire, but not in this rain. This was a man-made fire, but searching the surrounding area stealthily with my eyes revealed nothing but the empty forest. There was no sign of life anywhere, even a bird, but I knew very well someone was around to have made this thing. Advancing slowly towards it, I could make out a small clearing. In the centre, the fire continued to smoulder and crackle quietly and benignly. The smoke blew towards me, not upwards, the wind forcing a horizontal course for it amongst the trees, shunning the dull sky above. A large log turned on its side, next to a hollow stump, on the opposite side of the fire sufficed for a natural fireside seat. Yet there was no one about. No sound to betray the person who had made such a camp in this lonely spot. No footsteps, swishing through the dead leaves, warning me of the owner returning. No voices such as children would make, as if excited about their game of make-believe exploration and adventure. Nothing, nothing at all; just the fire and me and the rain. Someone must have made this fire, but when? How long ago? Could something like this smoulder unattended for hours, or even days? It seemed unlikely, so whoever had done this couldn't be far and might be returning at any minute. Was it a gamekeeper and was I on private land? Would he think I was a poacher and up to no good? Worse still came the thought that this campfire was the hiding place of someone who, up to no good or not, did not wish to be found, and who might not take kindly to being discovered. Warily, I peered around me, desperate to find where this person might be, so as to avoid stumbling upon them by accident, and just as desperate to remain hidden.

Perhaps it was that idea, of remaining hidden, or some other sixth sense, but I was suddenly awakened to that disquieting feeling which a human being has on sensing that they are being watched: of no longer being the hunter, but the quarry. I had heard nothing and seen nothing move, but perhaps had just been conscious of something, somewhere on the edge of my field of vision. The fact that I was not alone was verified sure enough by the presence of the fire, but the possibility of being watched, by a gaze unseen, gave me the desire to freeze that a wild animal has just before it darts off into the undergrowth. Perhaps that's what I should do, make a run for it. But that might mean running straight into the path of *that which watched.* My blue coat and jeans certainly were no disguise amongst these browns and greens, especially if I moved.

I can't say how long I must have been there, unable to move, fretful of discovery by person or persons unknown, anxious that even now I was being observed as I stood there, trying to decide what to do, where to go, not even knowing where I was. But staying there was not an option, and if this was some sort of stalemate, I wasn't going to wait for ever. Logic told me I had done nothing wrong, I was on a walk, had taken a wrong turn, lost my way, and was simply in need of finding a route back home. The longer I remained, indecisive, feeling guilty about stumbling on some other person's private space, the more I would look awkward and guilty. *Just walk on through. Act normal,* I told myself, *keep going and be decisive, don't creep about as if you are at fault! Head up, shoulders back! Walk!*

With such exhortations I forced myself from that place in the trees and advanced forward keeping the fire to my right and heading still steadily downwards. Eyes straight ahead, trying to look calm, ready to give a cheery *hello* to anyone I happened to stumble upon. Through gritted teeth I trudged, trying to keep my gaze natural from left to right, as if enjoying my afternoon stroll, still mindful of being studied from afar by invisible eyes.

I narrowly missed stepping on a dead blackbird

and found myself treading on a path. Possibly the one that led to the campfire, but it also led away from it, in the opposite direction, and figuring it must go somewhere, I walked, and kept on walking.

CHAPTER 16

When I awoke the following morning I saw white clouds scudding across a bright blue sky through the window above my bed. Half past nine. I had gone pretty much straight to bed on returning from my walk at about six o'clock, conscious of feeling feverish. I'd reached my front door with a raging headache, a sore throat and blocked sinuses. Two pints of water and some vitamin tablets was all I could face before I collapsed into a deep slumber. I ignored the house completely on my return, noting only, through the kitchen window that the back gate was once again wide open. Also, as I came into the front room, I saw that the glass on the ouija board had toppled over, still by the letter N, presumably from a gust created by slamming the front door when I had hurried out. Luckily it hadn't smashed.

The path that I had fortuned upon had lead me slowly downwards to the bottom of the wooded valley, where a muddy stream prattled nervously through the trees. I had followed the stream for about half a mile before the path crossed it, easy enough to jump over, and headed back up the other side of the valley. At some points the path had almost disappeared and I spent several minutes re-tracing my steps to find where it might have gone. Eventually it led me out of the woodland and onto some farmers' fields, but here again there seemed to be no public right of way, so I trekked around the crops in what I thought was an easterly direction. This proved to be false, for after half an hour of scaling gates and pushing through hedgerows I finally reached a metalled road, only a country lane, and not a signpost in sight to give me my bearings. Choosing to go left, I came at last to a junction, the sign at which pointed me back towards Poppington (five miles) by the way I had just come, so I turned tail and walked for forty minutes in the other direction, guessing at a couple of un-signposted forks, until at last happening upon a lane which came out behind Poppington Church. The rain had again abated to a damp drizzle. The village was quiet by this time; not a soul was about; the shop had long since shut, and the pub was yet to re-open for the evening's business. Not that I had wanted social refreshment, but I had long since finished my bottle of water, and the biscuits just made my throat even drier, so a fizzy drink would have perked me up no end for the final push to home.

As I lay there in bed, I cautiously swallowed to test my throat, and then slowly sat up to check if my head ached: both seemed back to normal. Breathing came easy, so the nose was back to rights too; maybe I had been dehydrated, or hungry, or tired. After two massive cups of tea, I retreated back to bed and dozed comfortably, cosy beneath the duvet. I remember dreaming that I was running through an open meadow. It was sunny and warm and as I kept running I got faster and faster. Instead of running out of energy, I seemed to gain more and more vigour, until, finally, effortlessly I stretched out my arms and took off into the air, soaring above the flowers and the trees and my own tiny house, far, far below - as if part of a model railway layout; and, like The Great Designer, I looked down upon my good little world.

Then I awoke, hungry for lunch.

After a shower, a tin of soup and lots of toast, I felt much more able to face the world, and took the car into Newstead to re-stock my food supplies from the local supermarket. I pondered going into the library, but decided against it for some reason and busied myself, on returning home, making a passable curry; maybe not good enough to serve to a guest, but perfectly OK for me.

The weather was much more clement; largely sunny but with a refreshing breeze, so it felt a lot less muggy than it had before the weather had broken. After dinner, the wind died down, and any clouds that were left melted away, leaving the rich blue sky to beckon an enchanting twilight. Too nice to be indoors, I found plenty of employment in the garden and began to dig over the border nearest the house, planning as I did, what sort of plants I would put here; Wasn't this where I had planned some fruit bushes? Redcurrants and raspberries perhaps? They would go with the wild blackberries I could see ripening in the hedgerow between the garden and the railway. I must have been inspired by the rows of canes in that picture in the library book (which I would have to return; maybe tomorrow?).

As I worked, giant bumble bees came and went, still happily foraging on the lavender that grew in the borders, their soft buzz adding to the delights of this sunny late spring evening. I imagined all those previous gardeners here, in this place, who had grabbed a quick moment to dig or prune during the lull between the bells that must have called them in to close the gates and set the signals for the oncoming trains. How different life must have been back then, when such a charming job came with its own accommodation in those labour-intensive days. No wonder the railways had had to cut costs just to survive. The cottage remained, but the crossing had closed long since, leaving the trains to bustle across the fields from station to station, gathering up people like clusters of pollen, before delivering them to the next place.

The digging had been invigorating, and only when I stopped did I feel the evening getting colder and darker. My watch told me it was past nine. Where had the day gone? The sun had set, although there was still plenty of light in the sky. The evening star was huge and brilliant, and faint dots of other stars were beginning to appear, as if in obeisance to it. A blackbird chirped his evening song from the apex of the roof, clear and distinct in the crispening air. Then he took flight and swooped off over the railway in search of his overnight roost. I followed him with my eyes until he was out of sight, and turned again to look up at the house, standing out bluntly against the darkening sky. I thought I saw a movement in the bedroom window and stood completely still, staring up at my room. For a moment or two my eyes could see nothing, but now I was sure I saw a movement again. I remained motionless, gazing and trying not to blink. Then, I saw, only for an instant, but unambiguously, a dark figure standing - inside my bedroom, at the window, looking out. I almost thought I saw a face, a woman's face, but just as I focused on her eyes, the figure dissolved into darkness, leaving me gazing at nothing.

Wondering if I had been deceived, or whether there might be someone in the house, I broke my stare by looking down at the claggy churned earth, then peered again, up at the window. Keeping my gaze fixed on the window, I began to walk slowly to the back door, hesitating as I reached it. Supposing there was an intruder inside. Would he or she be startled if I suddenly stumbled upon them as I went quietly in? I rattled the door noisily as if opening it to come in, went to shut it, and then thought better of it, in case I needed a quick means of escape. I switched on the kitchen light as I walked through to the back sitting room, stopping in the doorway just as before, when I had heard the footsteps from above. Pausing again, I held my breath and listened. Nothing: no noise. I picked up a large chopping knife from the worktop in the kitchen, before proceeding silently to the bottom of the stairs. I called out, "Hello. Is anybody there?" but was only answered by silence.

I peered into the front room. It was empty. The glass on the ouija board was still on its side by the letter N, untouched since I had come in yesterday. I checked the front door: still locked. I went to switch on the light at the bottom of the stairs, and once again, it pinged, almost silently, as the bulb blew. There must be something wrong with the fuse, I thought, because that was a brand new bulb. Or...

Then I began slowly to mount the stairs. I was suddenly overwhelmed again by my sense of isolation, my own helplessness, in this house, secluded from all others around it, by at least a mile of open countryside in every direction, all alone in a deserted world. Half way up, I heard a squeak. The door to the front bedroom must have moved. I didn't stop but went on upwards, automatically until I reached the top. In the dark, I could make out both bedroom doors, ajar, on either side of me, as I stood in that small enclosed space at the top of the staircase. I heard a mumble and stood, frozen, mechanically gripping the knife in my right hand. Then I heard it again, like the rasp of a whisper, coming from inside the front bedroom, behind the door to my left. Was it a whisper or was it a sob?

I switched on the light as I opened the door. The room was empty, but the curtain was swaying, even though no window was open. Carefully I surveyed the whole room, and my eye was drawn to the cupboard, the built in cupboard that jutted out over the stairwell. The same one where Sarah had seen the shadowy figure standing the night she slept in here. I walked over and tried the door, but it was stuck fast, as if locked from the inside. Strange, there was no lock on the inside of that door, I was sure. I paused, then went back to switch off the light. I had not been mistaken, for there in the crack under the door I could see a dim light. There was no light-fitting inside the cupboard either. I tried the door again. Still it would not yield. I pulled and tugged, but to no avail, grabbing harder as my frustration grew, switching the knife to my left hand and grasping the handle now with my right. Stopping to listen I held my ear up close to the door. It sounded as if I could hear breathing on the other side, yet I could not discern whether I was hearing anything but my own almost silent breaths. It was impossible to tell.

"Hello," I said. (I even knocked on the door.) "Is anyone in there?" I listened again, but in vain. "Is anybody there?"

Suddenly there was a slam and a door downstairs banged shut. I stopped pulling on the cupboard door and listened. Silence. I ran back downstairs to investigate, still clutching the knife. Going through the kitchen I saw that it must have been the back door, slamming in the wind. I couldn't detect any breeze outside, although it was difficult to tell for by now it was dark. I realised I was shaking. My hands were trembling like those of someone with a fever and I went straight to the kitchen cupboard and pulled down a bottle of whisky. I'm not a habitual drinker of such things. In fact this bottle was unopened, and, I think had been a gift from someone, years since, and I've no idea who it was from. Even so I needed something to calm my nerves. Pouring about a quarter of a tumbler, I downed it in one, and then poured another, just like people do in dramas on the television when they've had a shock. I'm not sure it helped. It tasted awful.

I went into the front room to fetch the laptop, but as I turned to go back into the kitchen, I saw that wretched glass on the ouija board, upright again, this time by the letter E. Stopping, staring, I wondered what this could mean. T-U-N-E. What could this be? I had already decided, whilst digging in the garden earlier, to clear this silly glass and the letters away, but now it seemed, something was being spelled out. But *TUNE*! What sort of a message began with a word like that?

Returning to the back room, I switched on the computer and searched the Internet for exorcisms. I'd had enough. This just had to stop. There wasn't much that I could readily find, but by now I was certain that these strange unexplainable happenings were linked to the house, and I needed to do something about it. My search revealed lots of useless information about films and their portrayal of exorcists, as well as tips for authors about writing such things. A few crackpots even offered to do exorcisms online, for a fee of course. Only one article drew my attention. It concerned a priest in the East Midlands who seemed qualified by the church, to be in charge of casting out evil spirits, and this was his role within the diocese. Elchester was a cathedral city and I wondered whether anyone fulfilled such a role in this area. The Elchester diocesan homepage did at least have a contact number for all general enquiries, so I wrote it down.

Feeling suddenly rather weary, I sat and drank two mugs of tea. After almost an hour of just sitting, gazing into space like some sort of zombie, my thoughts turned towards bed. A quick check of the garden revealed the gate to be wide open again. I shut it, and placed a large stone underneath it, to prevent it from re-opening. See what you make of that, I thought. I left the ouija board, with its glass still next to the letter E, wondering what the next letter in the conundrum would be, and retreated upstairs. The cupboard door in the front bedroom was still shut, but opened easily when I tried it. There was no sign of anything or anyone inside, or having been inside. Shutting the door, revealed no faint light gleaming from beneath, such as I had seen before. Catching sight of my weary, hollow face in the mirror whilst I undressed, I fancied I looked ten years older.

CHAPTER 17

On awaking the next morning I was indignant that I was not going to be beaten. No more was I going to creep about my own house, wondering hopelessly what was going on. It was time for action. I showered, did fifty press-ups, forty sit-ups, got dressed and sat down to write a list:

1. *Phone diocesan number.*
2. *See Belinda.* (To ask her out for lunch.)
3. *Ring Sarah.* (To tell her about the figure in the window, and the ouija board.)
4. *Find out who last lived at this address, and what happened to them.*
5. *Go to supermarket.*
6. *Buy padlock* (for the back gate.)
7. *Get more plants* (for the garden.)
8. *Find number of local vicar.*

I was pleased with my list. The things on it were in no particular order but just as they came into my head. It was nine o'clock, and I'd do some of the more straight forward things first, so I picked up my car keys and my wallet and set off for Newstead.

The sun was shining again, and although it was not so hot and humid as it had been, the forecast was for temperatures to climb again over the next few days. As I drove into town I felt my spirits lifting as if let out of some mental cage. I realised that some irrational fear of my own was driving me into this state of paranoia over the house, and the joy of finding myself jobless and with plenty of free time was also feeding this angst through having nothing else to worry about. As I drove on, I pictured Belinda, in her little house, tending to her house plants, then at the library helping old ladies to find their *Catherine Cooksons*, then at her mother's, her kind face gently, selflessly tending to everyone's needs. I decided I wanted some of that for myself. Such was the fantasy I had built up about her in my mind, as I parked the car outside the supermarket, plotting how I would ask her out to lunch, arrogant of my success and ignorant of anything going awry with my little plan. Still, it was all, at least, part of that new positive thinking that I had promised myself this morning.

But my hopes were dashed on discovering that Belinda wasn't in the library.

"I think she's at her mother's, down at the shop in Poppington," said Gwen with a giggle.

Not to be deterred, and before I thought better of it, I quickly dropped off my shopping at the house (no movement on either the ouija board or the gate - maybe that stone had done the trick) and jumped back into the car for the village.

To my surprise, Belinda was at the counter,

serving at the till. On the pretext of studying the shelf of tinned vegetables, I waited until she had finished serving a couple of locals, and when the coast was clear, dived in, placing my carefully considered tin of peas on the counter, asking whether or not they also sold frozen.

"You should look in the freezer over there," she said, somewhat standoffishly.

Not a promising start.

"Yes. I went to look for you earlier in the library, and Gwen said you'd be down here," I rushed. She smiled. "I was going to ask if you were free for lunch," I continued, "but maybe you're busy here?"

"Mum's ankles are playing up again, and she can't stand at the till all day, so I came down here to help her out."

"Not too bad I hope... her ankles, I mean... When will she better?"

"She needs to keep her foot up all week, so no time soon, I'm afraid."

"Will that mean you have to be here all week?"

"No, only today fortunately." She smiled again. "Mrs Snowdon from the village can manage the rest of the week, as she does when Mum's on holiday. It was just that she couldn't do today at such short notice, so I had to step in. Sorry about lunch. That would have been nice."

"Yes, oh well..." I wondered about plunging in and asking about tomorrow instead, but before I could, she said,

"Hold on a moment," and disappeared into the back. She was gone about a minute.

"Would you like to come here for dinner

tonight?" she asked as she came back. "It's only shepherd's pie, and you'll just have mother and me for company. Unless that is, you've got other plans?"

"No, of course not. If that's all right, I'd love to, thanks."

"It'll be something for Mum to look forward to, she's going stir crazy back there, unable to see anyone."

"I'll look forward to it too," I replied. "I've not had a chance to meet her properly. What time?"

"The shop closes at six, so how about seven?"

"Great," I said. "See you at seven." I turned to go. "Bye".

When I was half way to the door, she said, "Ed."

"Yes?" I turned round.

"Don't forget your peas."

I blushed as I went back to collect them, but she didn't seem to mind.

*

By the time we had finished the shepherd's pie, Mrs Taylor knew all about me: where I used to live, where I had worked, who my parents were, where they lived, even the places I'd been to on holiday. I got the feeling I was being vetted, yet had no idea if I was passing the test. Still she'd seemed pleased with the flowers I'd bought for her that afternoon during my visit to the garden centre. Her house, which appeared to be all but knitted to the back of the shop, was a quaint affair. There was one main sitting room, with a low ceiling, furnished with an old wooden dining table, a small sofa, an armchair and a large upright dresser, decorated with best plates and porcelain figurines of a seemingly bygone age. Delicate doilies served as scratch-savers, protecting the carefully polished surfaces beneath. The early evening sunshine sparkled through the net curtains, illuminating flowery wallpaper and matching vases brimming with red bouquets. An old piano had been pushed into the corner of the room. Several framed photos, dotted around, showed Belinda at various stages of growing up (two in school uniform, another with a tabby cat sitting on her lap), and one of a kindly looking gentleman I took to be Belinda's father. There was little space, but it oozed cosiness.

Then along came dessert (cherry crumble and vanilla ice cream). As Belinda was dishing it out, Mrs Taylor asked how I was getting on in my new house.

"Sorry about all the questions," interceded Belinda.

"I love living there," I said. I had decided not to mention the strange goings on, but seized the opportunity to find out more of the place's history. "I'm trying to find out about any of the previous occupants, but the place seems to have been empty for some time. Do you remember anyone who lived there, Mrs Taylor?"

"Well now, you're right of course, it's been empty for several years now. I think it was last lived in back in the seventies or eighties, I can't quite place when it was. Railway workers lived there, then, of course, only for a few months at a time, I believe, and it had long since stopped being a railway crossing. Now when did the crossing close? That must have been the fifties or sixties. Yes, that's it, the crossing closed in the sixties sometime, because it was during that time when - what's-his-name? - Beeching - made all his cutbacks, and there was even talk of the line here closing completely, all the way to Salthaven. Of course that never happened, they said something about freight on the line, and yes, the train still met with the boat to the continent: that didn't finish until the late sixties. So there was no question really of the line ever closing, but cost cutting meant we lost our station master, and porters, and I guess that was when they must have decided that it was easier to build a new access road to the farm and close the crossing. Yes, it was lived in for a few years after that, but I don't think I could tell you by who." She fell silent and gently cleared her throat, considering. She lifted a spoonful of her dessert, but paused before it got to her mouth. Then she began again; "But I do remember the tragic events of fifty-three."

"The train robbery."

"Yes," she said slowly, "the train robbery, and of course what happened next..."

"Do you mean Robert Wallace's arrest and execution?" I asked.

"That was how things were in those days, but it was a hard time for the village. The year of the Queen's coronation, which is why, I think, we were largely ignored by the rest of the country."

"How do you mean?"

"I shall tell you what I remember, but I was a young girl back then, and I do remember a lot of hushed whispers and black looks from nearly everyone in the village, so who knows after all these years which of my memories are accurate." She pondered a moment whilst she ate a spoonful of crumble. "No, Robert Wallace was a bad lot all round it seems. He was landlord of the pub as you probably know, but it wasn't the nice sort of pub it might be now. It was a sordid old place, dirty and unwelcoming, and only a few people ever really went in there, and they weren't the sort of characters most decent people wanted anything to do with. Yes, there were rumours of smuggling and all sorts back then."

"You mean drug smuggling?"

"Drugs, contraband, jewellery, forged notes... Yes he had a finger in a number of pies from what I can gather, none of them good. But most of that probably came to light later, after he was caught. Well, then there was his heist to hold up a train in the tunnel, using fake red lights. He robbed some poor Belgian, who got stabbed in the struggle, and then he went on the run. Of course, he could have been anywhere, but strangely enough, it turned out he was hiding in the woods a couple of miles outside the village, over towards Northgate Hill. Two weeks he managed to evade capture, and naturally when he was caught, everyone wondered who had helped him out (someone had been leaving food out for him, you see)... And who, or what, had kept him tied to this area, when he could have scarpered off up to Scotland, or disappeared into the underworld of London. But Wallace didn't run, he was waiting for something, or someone. At least that's what they said."

"The same person who had helped him out with the food, you mean."

"That was the general thought, yes. And then two weeks after Wallace was executed, and everything was just beginning to die down, Mrs Weston got herself killed by a train in the tunnel."

She paused, waiting for me to piece together the jigsaw.

"Suicide?" I asked.

"No one knew, but there wasn't much reason for her being in there, besides that."

"And she was the one who'd been helping Wallace out? She was his lover?"

"People put two and two together and came up with all sorts. But she was gone and she took her secrets with her. Needless to say, they never did catch Wallace's accomplice."

"Was there a Mr Weston?"

"There was indeed, but he was a lazy layabout, who did nothing all day except order his wife around. People said it was no wonder she looked for comfort elsewhere, if that's what she did. And maybe Wallace was where she looked. A ladies' man, for sure. Quite good-looking, if I remember - his picture was in all the papers. No one knew if it had been her, or someone else. But her husband, he knew what the rumours were, and soon sloped off. He couldn't bear the shame, some said, but no one seemed to think he was broken hearted at losing his wife. He lost his home anyway, when she died, so he *had* to leave." Mrs Taylor put down her spoon and gave me a sympathetic look. She smiled sadly.

"Who were they, these Westons?"

"Like I said, he was an idle, shiftless ne'er-do-well. She did all the work."

"What did she do?"

"Well, you see, *she* was the crossing keeper who lived in your cottage."

*

I lay awake that night thinking about what Mrs Taylor had said. The mention of Mrs Weston who had been the gate keeper at the crossing, back in 1953, gave me much to consider. After all, I had felt that it was a woman's face I had seen at my window the previous evening. Was my imagination trying to crowbar the story I had heard into the mysterious goings on at Railway Cottage? I thought and thought, over and over again, trying to conjure up in my mind's eye, just what I had seen from the garden. All I could remember was seeing a shape that had looked like a face, and even then only fleetingly. It could have been a trick of the light, naturally; or my eyes deceiving me. But had I not rushed into the house, convinced I had an intruder? And I had certainly felt the face was that of a woman *before* I had ever heard of Mrs Weston. And then the sight of this woman, whoever she was, had led to that freakish incident with the cupboard door, and I hadn't imagined that, had I? Was she Mrs Weston? Was the face at the window that of the old crossing keeper, some sixty years since? It must have been relatively unusual in those days, for a woman to have been a crossing keeper and not her husband, but then this had been shortly after the war, when I know a lot of women filled in for men who were called up to fight. Perhaps Mrs Weston kept her job on after the war? I wondered if I'd be able to find out more about their marriage from some old register or records. Perhaps they were local people?

Then there was her death. Suicide or not, being killed by a train was traumatic enough, and they did say spirits that haunted had usually met with some violent or unfulfilled end. It seemed likely that she could well have been Robert Wallace's illicit lover, cheating on a husband, who, for all I knew, had returned from the war a broken and demotivated man. Wallace sounded like the rogue of countless tales of villainy from times gone by... And the letters in the tin... Could they perhaps be...? Mrs Taylor had only been a young girl when all these events had happened, but the fact that even she had picked up on such things, at such a young age, meant there had to be some truth in it all, surely? Then there had been the detail about him hiding out in the woods, near Northgate Hill...

I jumped out of bed and ran downstairs to look at the Ordnance Survey map, wondering if I could locate Northgate Hill. Pouring over the area around the house, there it was, slightly to the north-west of the cottage; two miles at the most. And at the very same spot where I had got lost on my walk last Sunday. Where I had seen the unattended fire, and had that awkward feeling of being watched, whilst seeing no one about at all. Perhaps it wasn't the house the spirits were haunting; perhaps it was me. The notion that these strange happenings could follow me on my walk that day, had not occurred to me before now. I must be being totally ridiculous! I was tired and needed to sleep.

Too much thinking, I told myself. *Too much time on your hands. Always imagining the worst, and seeing horrors where there might be none. Think about something more positive.* And so I scolded myself as I slowly climbed the stairs, back up to bed.

But at least the telling-off might have worked, for I fell to sleep quickly, remembering insignificant, but pleasant things from the evening just gone: such as cherry crumble and vanilla ice cream... such as drying up the dishes, whilst Belinda washed up, side by side in the kitchen, whilst her mother had watched the television in the next room... such as that nice turn we had round the garden, as the evening light faded... such as the way she told me she would be free for lunch tomorrow...

CHAPTER 18

After a good night's sleep, with no happenings out of the ordinary, I was up early and the bright and breezy morning held my mood. I fitted the padlock to the back gate, tidied the house, and rang Sarah, only to find she wasn't in, because I'd stupidly forgotten she would be at work. I then tidied the house even more, no doubt because I was excited about meeting up with Belinda for lunch, and couldn't sit still. I cleared away the ouija board, as if to symbolically put an end to any more spiritualistic nonsense. The glass had moved no more since settling on the E of TUNE, whatever that was supposed to have meant, so it went back in the cupboard and the pack of cards back in their box, on the shelf by the front door for Sarah to collect when she next visited.

To avoid running the gauntlet of Gwen's inane gawping, Belinda met me in the market place and we went to a nice little bistro that I'd not yet discovered. Newstead appeared to have plenty of hidden delights if only one knew where to look. We sat on the patio out the back, and soon fell to discussing all sorts of things, finding out more about one another, discovering, for instance that neither of us were particularly ambitious career-wise, and like me, she didn't have a television, thinking watching one a waste of time. She did have a passion for the theatre, a subject on which I was virtually ignorant. But then she couldn't ride a bike, and had no interest in learning to either.

She had been an only child, and had been brought up in Poppington in her parents' shop, doing well enough at school to move away to university in London. She had returned home after qualifying as a Library and Systems Manager, because her father suddenly became ill, and when he died shortly afterwards, didn't feel she could abandon her mother, although she reckons in hindsight that her mother would have coped very well. Somewhere, deep down, she speculated, maybe she hadn't wanted to leave at all. The job of managing Newstead Library, for which she was rather over-qualified, had come up and she had taken it, temporarily, she had thought, whilst her mother got back on her feet. However, gradually a few months became a year, the year became two years, and now it had been ten years since her father had died and she'd never moved on. Partly, she said, she regretted this, but another part of her recognised that she had relatively few needs, and an enjoyable, if unexciting lifestyle, which had so far prevented her meeting someone to settle down with. She had, she said with a smile, even begun to contemplate a life of spinsterhood.

This brought the conversation round to me, and I went to similar lengths to explain why I was still single, trying at one and the same time to neither sound too sad and desperate, nor too forward and brazen. After what I felt was ample circumventing, I asked her what she was doing on Friday evening. Was she free to come round for a meal? Friday, as it turned out was a visit to Leonie and Vikki's, long-since pre-arranged, but could she be cheeky and ask if the offer was still open for Saturday? Of course it was, I beamed, and suddenly, it was half past two, and Belinda said that Gwen would think she was taking liberties, and that she must hurry back.

The next few days passed by pleasantly enough. I had no more unexplainable incidents, and the weather continued to get hotter, the mercury hitting the high twenties Celsius. Grateful not to be stuck in a classroom in this heat, I busied myself about the house and garden and took the opportunity in the cool of the morning to venture out on my bike, discovering new country lanes as the swifts screeched overhead and the landscape slowly baked once more.

An electrician actually came round the very same day I phoned (unheard of!) and managed to fix the oven. I planted some small redcurrant bushes in the garden, perhaps unwise at this time of the year, but with a bit of luck and a lot of water, I was hopeful of a tasty crop for next year. I mended the water butt, and transferred all the old boxes from the bedroom cupboard up to the loft, yanked up the kitchen lino and scrubbed the flagstone floor underneath until you could eat your dinner off it. The darker floor made the kitchen seem slightly smaller, but the stones were nice and cool underfoot in the heat of the afternoon.

Considerably unpractised at entertaining a "date", I had a go at a chicken and pecan dish on Thursday evening to check that it worked for Saturday, and the results were really rather delicious. I returned to the garden centre again on Friday to purchase a new garden dining table and chairs, and bought some bags of gravel to cover some of the less delightful areas of the garden. It would do until I got round to re-grassing or laying a patio. I stood there, outside the back door, on Friday evening, arms folded, very pleased with my efforts.

*

She knocked at the door, clutching a bottle of wine, at five past seven on Saturday evening. Dinner was happily bubbling in the oven and we sat out the back, the sunshine still warm, whilst she said complimentary things about my gardening efforts.

"The last time I was here, you were covered in muck and arranging these stones over here."

"Yes," I replied. "If I had never lost my wallet, I wouldn't have met you. How was Vikki and Leonie's last night?"

"Oh it was fine. Ian and Kate were there too. Vikki said I should have invited you along."

This was a good sign, since it meant I had come up in conversation. "How long have you known them?" I asked.

I'm not sure I listened to the answer. I was too busy watching her sip her wine and unconsciously push a curl of dark hair back that kept falling across her face. She chatted away with ease, but without smiling too much, and I began to wonder whether the signs I had read had all been in my imagination. Is it too early to say something intimate? I wondered. When does one say that sort of thing anyway? Should I wait till next time I see her? Or, if I wait, will she think I'm not interested? I felt so hopelessly out of practice: too many years had rolled by since I'd last asked a girl out. Wasn't I too old for this sort of thing now? What if I get those dreaded words *I'm sorry but I don't think of you in that way*? Would I then be more sorry to think that she was out of reach, and I was not in her league, or would I be more sorry about my own wounded pride? And suddenly I began to question whether or not I wasn't just lonely.

Too many questions, and too over-analytical as usual. *Just enjoy the evening and see what happens!*

"...they liked you, you know, and so did Ian and Kate." I had tuned back in to what she was saying in time for a compliment.

"And Gwen? Does she like me too?" I smiled.

"Oh, I think so. She just has a funny way of showing it. But you *were* a big hit with my mother. *Such a nice young man!*" she mimicked.

All these compliments! Surely I hadn't read the signs so wrong?

Chatting away over dinner was easy and there were no awkward silences. She told me all about her job, and some of the bizarre things that had happened, during her time at the normally quiet and pedestrian library: such as the day someone had died in the large print section, and the day an irate lady had found a pornographic video inside a case that should have contained a film about a tour of stately homes in England.

Over dessert, talk got round to the house and I found myself telling her all about the mysterious movements of objects, the chalk crosses, the back gate, the letters in the tin, the ouija board and the cupboard upstairs. She listened to my idea about Mrs Weston and Robert Wallace with interest, but admitted to being sceptical about ghosts and hauntings. She wanted to be open-minded, but all these things usually had a logical explanation, even though she did fail to explain some of my happenings. Ghost stories were for children, and she had never yet read one that had actually frightened her. I began to wonder whether this had been a wise topic of conversation. I was merely making myself look stupid, in front of someone I was keen to impress, so tried to veer the conversation towards a different subject - anything - even the weather.

Luckily it was a beautiful, calm evening. The sun gently set behind the house and we were interrupted only by the evening song of the blackbird and the rumble of trains as they clattered past the locked gate at the end of the garden. As darkness fell, I lit some candles and an old lantern I'd found whilst unpacking. A hedgehog trundled across the garden, oblivious to our presence and captivating us both as it snuffled through the beds and around the stones.

"I must say, you have a beautiful home," she

said at last. "So peaceful and isolated. I feel I could sit here forever. Thanks for such a lovely evening."

Her eyes, all of a sudden, had that glassy, faraway look; as if the occasion had just reminded her of a different time and she was gazing upon some foggy memory through a distant haze.

"Well... I was wondering what you'd say, if I asked you stay."

There! I'd said it. I hadn't planned to, but just spontaneously blurted it out.

Immediately, I felt I was speaking too soon, and immediately I wished I had waited longer before charging in, where, as they say, angels fear to tread. Suddenly I wanted the ground to open up and swallow me. What a fool I was, to tarnish such a charming evening. I held my breath, waiting for a reply, looking down at my empty dish, not wanting to look up into those dark eyes and see a look of pity and rejection. I listened. Only the blackbird spoke. Finally, I couldn't stand it any more and looked up at her across the little table in the dying evening light.

She smiled, when she saw me look up. "Ah," she said and paused. "Then I wouldn't have to think about going."

CHAPTER 19

Once again, I awoke with a start. The red digital numbers of the bedside clock radio read *two: forty-six.* Another sultry night, and for a moment nothing seemed wrong, until of course I remembered that Belinda should have been beside me. The bed was empty apart from myself. I slid across and looked down. Her dress was not on the floor where we had playfully left it a few hours before. I don't know if I felt surprised, piqued or angry. Had she gone? If so, why? Surely I hadn't been that bad! Then I saw her phone on the bookshelf. If she had gone, she'd left that behind. Perhaps she had just got up for a drink. There wasn't a breath of air, and the warm humid night hung about the house like a thick suffocating blanket. I could do with a glass of water myself. Stepping out of bed, I walked out onto the landing.

"Belinda?" I called. There was no answer. The house felt empty, and despite the stifling airless heat, I felt an involuntary shiver. Walking through to the front bedroom I looked out of the window. Belinda's car was still parked outside, next to my own. This should have offered me some comfort. She hadn't dumped me in the middle of the night after all. I hadn't been jilted after one night of rare passion, and that might have made me grateful. Yet I had a funny feeling that it wasn't good news at all. The house just felt so empty. Even my bare feet on the bedroom rug had a dull echo to them that I had never noticed before.

"Belinda!" I called again.

Maybe she'd gone into the garden. I turned round and noticed that dull glow from the cupboard door again. Reluctantly, I went over and tugged at the door. Once more it wouldn't budge, as if something was holding it from the inside: Something much stronger than myself.

"Belinda?" My voice sounded weaker this time. More futile. Back in my bedroom, I pulled on the pair of shorts and short sleeved shirt that I'd worn earlier in the evening. I stopped to throw on a pair of trainers too, I don't really know why. Just in case.

As I trotted down the stairs, I called her name again, trying to sound jovial, in case I found her there, sipping a glass of water, but somehow I just knew I wouldn't. I switched on the light at the bottom of the stairs. This time it did not ping out and I stooped down to pick up a little piece of white card from the floor, which I had only just noticed. Turning it over, I realised that this was one of those cards from the *Lexicon* game that Sarah had brought round. I thought that I had put them all back in the box, yet this one seemed to have gone astray, only to turn up now. How odd! I put my head round the door of the front room to see if Belinda was in there, (perhaps fallen asleep on the sofa, to escape my snoring?) but there was no sign of her. Also, to check on the pack of cards, which were still where I had left them. I placed the stray card on the top of the pack, barely noticing as I did so that it was the letter L, and strode through to the kitchen.

The back door was shut, but unlocked, as I had left it, and grabbing the torch I went out into the garden.

"*Belinda!*" I hissed. I don't know why I whispered it. Somehow it didn't seem right to bellow her name out into the still dark night. Letting my eyes become accustomed to the torchlight, I scanned the garden. Still no sign of her. But the back gate was wide open. I stopped, trying to piece together what was going on. Belinda's car was still here, but she was not. Her dress was gone but not her phone. The back gate was open. Maybe she had sleep-walked off down the railway line... Unless...

There was no way she could have found the key to the padlock, asleep or awake. It was hidden in the kitchen drawer amongst the cutlery. On closer examination I could see that the padlock had simply vanished. It wasn't hanging there unlocked. Nor had it been smashed by some vandal and left in pieces on the ground, either in the garden or on the steps down to the tracks. It had just gone...

All these thoughts were whirring through my head much quicker than it takes to write them, and almost instantaneously another idea emerged which I also had to consider. Hadn't that wretched glass on the ouija board fallen over on the letter N? Could that have meant N twice? And with the letter L, would that not now spell *TUNNEL*? This fanciful idea bubbled up in my head as I surveyed the missing padlock and open gate. In fact, it seems now, that maybe I'd even begun to realise this as I had placed the letter L back on top of the pack in the front room. The entreaties I made to myself to *stop being so silly* just didn't seem to have any credence, no matter how far-fetched the alternative seemed. The tunnel. The place where Mrs Weston had met her end. The open gate. Belinda missing. I seemed to be adding up small numbers and coming up with an enormous one, but I just could not push my mind towards another solution.

I looked down the tracks, in the direction of the tunnel. I could see nothing except the parallel lines of steel stretching away around the corner to that dark cavernous abyss beyond. I knew what this meant. I knew what I was going to have to do. I shouted this time: "*Belinda!*" When my call was unanswered by the empty night, I set off warily down the barren tracks.

*

A fierce, warm wind began to blow. The scanty moon appeared now and then in the gaps between the racing, ominous clouds. I rounded the corner and saw the tunnel entrance looming up in front of me. I won't say I ran, for I'm not a runner, but I jogged as best as I could trying not to trip on the sleepers or the ballast. Three o'clock in the morning: There shouldn't be any trains around, but, I'd been caught out in that way before. I paused at the tunnel entrance, wondering whether or not to proceed inside, catching my breath, thinking that this could just be a folly too far. Belinda was probably back in the house, sipping that glass of water, wondering where on earth I was. Perhaps I should go back after all.

The cupboard, the letter L, the open gate and the missing padlock; these were the things that had driven me here, and incredulous as it sounded, I just couldn't go back. Shouting her name once more, I listened as my voice echoed down the dark cavern. Nothing but my own tapering voice, or was that a quiet distant sob that I just heard? I called again, and heard the same response, unsure if it was part of my own echo or someone else. Somewhere in the dark a final answer was beckoning, taunting me and my attempts to solve this riddle. Stepping forward I reached into the empty gulf and was swallowed up by the black void. I switched on the torch. It did nothing to dispel my fear, in fact I half wondered if the darkness wasn't preferable. Ignorance is bliss, but in the torchlight the tunnel seemed more forbidding than ever; a shroud of darkness luring me towards lurking horrors, like the lair of some giant, morbid, funnel-like web.

The brick walls rose beside me like those of a mighty tomb, and my footsteps began to resound off them as I ventured deeper and deeper inside. The wind ceased. The temperature dropped. It felt colder, damper. By this time I was walking, my confidence waning with every step, no longer brave enough to jog. My heart told me to press onwards, my common sense, all the time, urging me back towards the open air.

"Belinda!" I called again. "Are you in here?"

I waited. That sobbing sound seemed yet more distinct, but I was not sure what it actually was.

"Belinda!" I cried, pacing steadily on, "Belinda!"

Then I heard it. Definitely a voice: Quiet, sobbing. "Help me. Help me." Not an exclamation, but a mournful plea.

"I'm coming. Is that you, Belinda? I'm coming. Don't worry. I'm nearly there."

Two eyes pierced the darkness. Not the eyes of a human, but green and reflective in the torchlight. I froze as they fixed on me. They seemed to freeze too. Staring as two pinpoints out of nowhere. Then they seemed to be getting closer. For the next few seconds I held my breath, transfixed as they came towards me, and all of a sudden they disappeared from view as a shape passed by, rapidly, just above knee height, over on the opposite track. The torch picked out a bushy tail, and I breathed a sigh of relief: a fox.

"Where are you?" I called down into the depths of the tunnel. I could make out a small red light now. Bigger than the fox's eyes, and all on its own. It must be a signal, a red light to stop the trains, I thought, without thinking that the middle of a tunnel would be a rather unusual place to put a such a signal.

"Help me!" came the voice again, more urgent this time, but still faint. "Come closer!" It seemed to be coming from the red light, which was dim, but, I guessed about two or three hundred yards ahead.

"I'm coming," I said. "Can you see my torch?"

"Yes, come here. Who is that?"

"It's me, Ed. Is that you, Belinda?"

I walked on listening.

"Don't come any nearer!" Suddenly the voice was harsh and menacing. "Why did you bring me here?"

Despite being ordered to stop, I kept walking, slowly, until a figure appeared in the beam of the torch.

Belinda was lying on the right hand track, her face arching up towards me, her dress tattered and torn. She was lying on her front, but supported herself on her hands, so that she could face me.

"What do you mean, *why did I bring you here*?" I asked.

"What are you? Some sort of pervert, who lures women into his bed, only to imprison them in some sort of dungeon?"

"I didn't bring you here. I woke up, and you were gone, so I came to look for you."

"You expect me to believe that! I've heard about men like you, capturing women, and keeping them imprisoned for years and years, whilst you rape and abuse them." I stepped forward. "Don't come any closer!" She hurled a handful of stones at me.

"Hey!" I exclaimed, as one of the stones caught me on the forehead. Nevertheless, I didn't step any closer. "Well if that's what you think you're free to go. The way out's that way." I pointed the torch back down the tunnel. "If you want to think I've imprisoned you in here, then you're free to go."

"Where is this place anyway?"

"It's the railway tunnel, along the line at the end of my garden. Three minutes that way and you'll be out in the open. Three more minutes and you'll be by the garden gate."

"You think I'm stupid! A railway tunnel!"

"Yes, look." I shone the torch light on the steel tracks.

"How could I possibly have got here?" she spat incredulously.

"That's what I want to know. Do you sleep walk?"

"Sleep walk! What are you? Some sort of idiot? Some sort of mad-man?"

"Well, how did you get here?"

"Stop acting the innocent. You know perfectly well how I got here."

"No I don't. And as I said, you're free to go."

Another stone whizzed past my face. I ignored it. I stood waiting for her to go.

"I can't go, you shit, I've sprained my ankle. Why do you think I'm lying here like this?"

"Well, I'll have to carry you out then."

"Don't come any closer. Don't touch me, you bastard." Another stone flew at me. "I'll get out by myself, if I have to drag myself out on all fours."

"No you won't, it might be broken. You'll have to let me help you." Another stone flew at me. This one hit me on the nose. "Stop throwing those stones at me. Here let me help you up."

"Keep away!" she screamed, tears streaming down her face. "I'm not throwing any stones. Stop playing games with me!"

Her voice was desperate now. She seemed convinced that I was her captor, and I had no way of convincing her otherwise.

"Shhh!" I silenced her shouting, but then she started sobbing. I stood still and shone the torch over her head and further down the tunnel. Another stone flew. This one hit Belinda on the head. "Something down there is throwing stones at us," I said. "They seem to be coming from that red glow." Standing there for a further minute, two more stones pinged towards us out of the darkness. Belinda continued crying quietly, her face now buried in her hands. "Tell me what you remember," I said. She didn't answer, so I repeated the question.

"What do you mean?" she wailed.

"Do you remember getting up?"

"What is this? You want to relive the story of your kidnap for some sort of sadistic pleasure whilst I recount your crimes for you. Is that how you get your kicks?"

"Listen, I told you strange things had been going on in my house. I didn't bring you here. Why would I? If I wanted to keep you a prisoner, I'd have locked you in the bathroom! What do you remember, from the moment we were in bed? Did you wake up in here?"

"Oh how very convenient, trying to make this sound like one of your stupid haunting stories. What do you take me for?"

"What do you remember?" I asked again, ignoring her. "I don't want to believe it either. Did you wake up here in this tunnel?"

"You know perfectly well what happened, you did it." Her voice was slightly calmer now, as if she was unsure of herself, and had begun to think that maybe there was something in what I had said.

"Tell me. Humour me." I conjectured, trying to sound sarcastic, as if none of her accusations mattered to me. "I followed you here, because when I went looking for you in the garden, the padlock was gone and the gate was open." I didn't tell her about the card with the letter L on it, as I didn't want to stretch her credulity too far. There was a long pause. Another stone flew and clattered into the ballast about a foot behind me. "See!" I said. "Something odd's going on..."

She seemed to be thinking it all over, and maybe she began to suppose that if I was telling the truth, it was a better bet than trying to fight me, with a broken ankle, in a railway tunnel. Finally, she said quietly; "I got up for a drink of water. I was hot. You were fast asleep, snoring. I didn't want to wake you. I wandered through into the front bedroom to look out of the window. I don't know why. When I turned to go back down the stairs, I saw a strange glow of light coming from the cupboard in the corner of the room. I went over to the door, opened it. Then... you... something... pushed me through the doorway. I fell, hit my head and came to in here." She sobbed again. "My ankle hurts so much. I tried to stand on it but just fell over... Then I saw a light coming and heard someone calling. I was frightened, petrified. I couldn't think where I was..." she trailed off, as if hardly believing it herself.

Next there was a louder noise as something

larger landed between us. The ballast rattled and a few stones sprang up with the impact. It was a brick, presumably one that lined the tunnel. Whatever was throwing the stones was now upping its game, and I didn't want to hang around much longer to see what would come our way next.

"See," I said. "I didn't throw that and nor did you. Come on let's get out of here." Resting the torch on the rails, I leant down to pick Belinda up. "I'll give you a piggy-back," I said. "Will your ankle be ok?"

Her only answer was to pull herself up slowly, wincing if she even so much as touched her left foot on the ground, so I guessed she assented. I picked up the torch and crouched down so she could climb on my back. As I straightened up I became filled with horror. A deep rumbling sound and a humming of the rails betrayed the approach of a train. I looked up to see the headlights of the approaching train coming into the tunnel from the direction which I had walked.

"Oh my God!" Belinda whispered over my shoulder.

"It's ok," I said, trying to stay calm. "It'll be on the other track. We just have to wait here until it passes. I'm going to move to the side a bit and hope we don't get seen by the driver. Look away from the train, towards the wall, so that we're less likely to be visible." I shuffled over to the side of the tunnel to wait for the train to pass. It seemed to be approaching rather slowly. The noise increased. Something didn't quite seem right. Turning to face down the tunnel in the opposite direction to the approaching train, I realised what was wrong. Another train was approaching from that direction too. No wonder the din was so loud. Now it was my turn.

"Oh shit," I said. Belinda must have turned and seen the impending horror too, for I heard her gasp. Standing on one track to avoid a passing train was one thing, but with two approaching, one from each direction, neither track offered safety from the other. The only choice seemed to be, which track to stand on and die. The tunnel wall trapped us and I was almost certain the clearance on either side was going to be minimal. If we tried it and were wrong there'd be no second chance. With the trains approaching, there was no time to make a decision. No time to consider which side of the tunnel might offer more room as the train passed on that particular track. No time to think, whether one train would arrive before the other one and we could leap from one track to the other as the first passed to avoid the second. No way of telling how long the trains were, nor how fast they were moving.

If I thought of all this at the time it was in a momentary split second.

"We'll have to lie down on the ground, between the two tracks," I blurted out, "and let both trains pass by us."

Without waiting for an answer I lowered Belinda down into the space between the two railway tracks, and I'm sure her ankle must have been screaming with pain, being bundled down on the ballast quickly like that, but I guess she too realised it was our only choice. I covered her head as best I could with my arms, as I laid beside her pressing my body into the stones to make us as low as possible. There was no time to shallow out a little hollow for us to lie in.

With a roar, the train that we had seen first thundered overhead, but it only just beat the second train, which seemed to be travelling faster. My eardrums felt set to burst, as the noise of the diesel engines, the dust and the incredible force of air battered us from above. It was as if the trains were bearing down on us. Tons of steel were turning on tons of steel, just inches from my face. Murmuring some sort of expletive, or a prayer, as I shut my eyes tighter than I've ever shut them before, I buried my face in the stones and feared for the end.

As the second train finished thundering over us, a massive thud on my back made me truly think my time had come. The first train, longer and slower than the second (probably a freight, though I didn't take the time to look), eventually passed and in the receding noise, I could hear my laboured breathing, until we were left in darkness, with the gentle humming on the rails tapering away.

"Belinda, are you ok?"

She didn't answer.

Slowly reaching behind my back, still lying down, my hands touched a large brick which had landed there. I cautiously manoeuvred it off and slowly inched myself up onto my knees, tentatively checking whether any bones were broken. Scratches and bruises, yes, but broken bones no. I had been lucky. The dropped torch could not be found in the darkness, so I fumbled in my pocket for a lighter, relieved that I had lit those candles earlier. Flicking the flame I knelt down to see how Belinda was. She seemed to be breathing, gently, but had passed out. I checked for signs of blood as best as I could, and was relieved to find none. I hoped she had fainted, rather than being knocked out by a flying brick to the head. I couldn't see any bricks in the vicinity, except the one that had landed on me. As I passed the lighter over it, the single flame revealed a white chalky cross on it, reminiscent of the ones that had appeared on my bedroom floor, all those days ago.

"Belinda!" I called softly, hoping to wake her up. Still no response.

Resting my thumb a little, I re-lit the lighter and held it up in front of me to see a bit more. My eyes were full of grit, and I had to stop myself from rubbing them, having no water to hand. I blinked repeatedly, which seemed to help. As I opened my eyes properly, I saw a gap in the tunnel wall, the shape of a brick, and perhaps the place from which my missile had fallen. It was about head height, and in the pathetic light of the small naked flame it seemed as if a mouse peered down at me from the little hole. Clearly a trick of the shadows, but an odd looking one, nonetheless. The mouse didn't move, so I reached my fingers towards it. When I touched it, I flinched away in disgust. It was a mouse, or a small rat, I could feel its soft body, but it was cold and dead and lifeless. It fell to the floor as I abruptly withdrew my hand, but made a sound as it fell, which made me stop, because a dead mouse would surely hit the stones with no detectable noise, even with the tunnel acoustics.

Relighting the lighter, with my other thumb I took a closer look. Possibly it wasn't a mouse at all. It was dark and soft, maybe brown or black or dark blue; impossible to tell in this dim light. It was a little cloth bag, about three inches long. As I touched it again, I could feel something hard and solid inside.

I stuffed it into my pocket and knelt down again beside Belinda. She murmured softly as I gently touched her face, my finger smoothing her cheeks, to see if this gentle stimulus might revive her. She made an incomprehensible sighing sound, but nothing more. At least this stupor would be numbing the pain of her ankle.

I don't know how I did it, but I managed to carry her out of the tunnel, back along the tracks, through the garden gate, and into the house using some form of fireman's lift. Adrenalin must have helped. When I laid her down on the couch, my back, my legs and my arms were all bursting with pain. Belinda looked an absolute mess, but then so did I. She hadn't come round fully, but perhaps that had been a blessing whilst carrying her out of the tunnel. After what she had said about me kidnapping her, to have awoken whilst I was carrying her off, literally over my shoulder, might have reminded her of all those previous fears which she had so eloquently expressed when I had found her. I wasn't sure how much she would still think like this, when she came to.

I splashed a little water over my face, drank some water to quench my raging thirst, and then wiped Belinda's face with a damp cloth, cleaning some of the muck out of the scratches, as I went.

"I'm going to put you in the car and take you to the hospital." I said, unsure if she could really hear me. At the sound of my voice she made a few soft murmurs herself, but still said nothing coherent. I kept uttering soothing little comments whilst I quickly gathered my wallet and keys together, before scooping her up again and belting her into the front seat of my car.

The nearest hospital with an A&E, was in Wilthorpe, and I knew well enough where it was because it was only round the corner from my old house in Avenue Green. At this time of the morning, it would not take more than thirty minutes to get there. I just worried how Belinda would react, if she woke up to find me driving her at speed through the countryside. And what I was going to tell the hospital staff, I had no idea.

CHAPTER 20

Luckily I was spared both these dilemmas. On arrival at the hospital, Belinda was still not lucid, and a hospital porter, who was having a crafty smoke in the car park during the quiet hours of the early morning, saw my predicament of getting her from the car and into the building, and went straight inside to fetch a bed-trolley. Beyond wanting to know the patient's name and where her injuries were, the hospital staff who took over as we entered, seemed content enough when I told them she had fallen down some steps, through an open gate. Whilst not the truth at all, it seemed to me to be some sort of reasonable compromise.

They took Belinda away and I was left waiting. Hospitals always depress me, so I wandered outside.

The chrome dawn brushed gently upwards into a powdery sky. This was one of those beautifully fresh, cool early summer mornings that promised a warm, but not muggy, day to come. The fierce wind of the night before had died down; the threatened storm had not materialised.

As I stood there in that car park, wondering what to make of it all, people arrived for work, or waited at the bus stop opposite, in their everyday, mundane sort of way. I must say, I watched them with a tinge of envy. Maybe I was too young for this retirement lark. I needed a job, a career, something to occupy my mind other than all these ridiculous, supernatural puzzles.

After about an hour's wait, it was nearly seven o'clock and a nurse told me that the doctor would see me shortly.

"She's got mild concussion and a broken ankle," Doctor Raman said placidly. "You're not her husband, her next of kin, are you?"

"No. I'm just a friend."

"Would you be able to notify...? Who would be her...?"

"...her next of kin would be her mother," I said. "There's nothing to worry about is there?"

"No not at all, it's just that we have to know who to speak to when a patient is unable to speak themselves. She's already started to come to, but we want to keep an eye on her, check her vision and so forth, before we let her go. We'll keep her in for most of the day, and sort out the ankle. That'll have to go in a brace. She might be ready to go home tonight, but it would be better if she stayed with someone for a few days, like her mother..."

"I could go and fetch her mother?"

"Yes that would be good idea. Just leave her details and yours with the nurses at the desk before you go."

*

Fortunately the shop was empty. The bell announced my arrival as I pushed open the door. Mrs Taylor took the news very calmly when I told her that Belinda was in hospital with concussion and a broken ankle, and that I was ready to drive her there. She gave me a look, which meant something like *What have you been doing with my daughter?* but merely said, "Thank you. Could you just mind the shop whilst I give Mrs Snowdon a ring and find my things?"

I heard her rummage about in the living room, getting her coat etc. After making a short phone call, she came back through.

"Gayle can only do a couple of hours, so I'll just tell her to close early when she needs to be off, because I don't know when we'll be back. She should be able to come home this evening, you say?"

"Yes, hopefully, and she'll probably need to stay here for a day or two, while she recuperates."

"Luckily we close at twelve on Sundays," she said, "so Mrs Snowdon will at least see most of the Sunday papers get to the right people."

We both stood there, waiting awkwardly in silence. Belinda's mother looked far calmer than I felt. I gazed pointlessly at my shoes, then at a shelf full of tinned fruit, then back at my feet. Finally the bell jangled as the door opened.

"Don't you worry, Mrs Taylor," said a voice bustling into the shop. "I'll take care of everything in here 'til about half ten, and after that our Laura can go round on her bike and deliver any papers as haven't been collected." This was clearly the reliable Mrs Snowdon. Already, she was taking off her heavy brown overcoat. "You get yourself up to that hospital and see how your Belinda is, don't you worry 'bout a thing here. Off you go now."

"Thank you, Gayle, you're marvellous," said Mrs Taylor, and we went outside to the car.

*

The nurse directed us to Room 4B, and as we reached the end of the corridor and rounded the corner, I could see Belinda through the glass partition, sitting up in bed, looking a bit bruised and forlorn, but capable enough to sip a glass of water. I held back and let her mother go in. I decided to hover out of sight just down the corridor. I was almost certain that Belinda would still see me as some sort of dastardly scoundrel. Unsure of the reception I would get, I did not want to hang around for another tirade. I thought I might just check Mrs Taylor didn't want anything, before I headed off, though how I would do that, without seeing her daughter, I wasn't sure.

"Belle!" I heard her mother say as she went round the partition and over to her daughter's bed. "What have you done?" I couldn't hear Belinda's reply, but there was a lot of murmuring going on.

"Ed!" Belinda called.

I sheepishly stuck my head round the partition. "Hi."

"Come on over," she beckoned with her hands,

as well as her eyes, and her smile seemed to be indicating that all was forgiven. "Mum, I've been terribly silly. Ed was kind enough to invite me over for a meal, and I'm afraid I had too much wine, got drunk and fell through the gate, down some steps in his garden." (She must have spoken to Dr Raman). "I fell on the railway tracks, and broke my ankle. Then a train came along and I thought I was going to get killed, but Ed rushed over and rescued me. Mum, what an idiot I am. I'm sorry if I worried you... and I've made you leave the shop... and I've ruined Ed's evening, and... Oh I'm so sorry, both of you!"

Mrs Taylor perched on the bed and clucked sweet remonstrances at her daughter. *Everything was all right, no real harm done, you young people always getting into scrapes, just as long as you've learnt a lesson, we all do silly things...* etc.

Belinda looked up at me and smiled. I wondered what she saw and I hoped that my admiration for her might somehow be reciprocated. It struck me that here was someone mindful enough to humbly fashion the whole trauma into an apology, when all along *she* had been the unwitting victim of... well, who knew what?

I stood by her bedside as they chatted away, gradually finding myself filling in any gaps in Belinda's story, pleased to no longer be regarded as a fiendish kidnapper, but exceptionally tired, and beginning to show it.

"Ed you must go home and get some rest!"

"Well I could do with a bath and a nap," I admitted. "But I'm coming back at four to take your mum home, and hopefully you too. They should discharge you then, or shortly afterwards."

"No you don't have to do that; we can get a taxi," protested Mrs Taylor.

"I'd like that very much," said Belinda.

"Belle...!" Mrs Taylor was about to argue.

"No, I insist," I said, and gave Belinda a grin as she beamed back.

*

The warm sunshine hugged me as I left the building. Spring this year had certainly been a bewildering succession of early heat waves. I sauntered across the car park and wearily fumbled for my keys, psyching myself up to stay awake for the journey back to Poppington. As I did so, a small cloth bag fell from my pocket, landing at my feet. I leant down to pick it up. It didn't look anything like a mouse. I smiled ruefully.

Without opening it, I already knew, that inside, I would find some diamonds.

CHAPTER 21 - DEPARTURE

The air is cold and tickles my lungs as I breathe in. I have just finished clearing the snow, making sure that there is a way from the lane to park a car outside the front of the house. There is not much of a covering, but it looks beautiful in the fading light. As I go back through the front door I pause to look at the thick flakes drifting serenely down. To clean my boots, I gently tap them on the doorstep and allow the warmth of the room to envelope me once again. The Christmas tree is finally up and there are some carols playing on the radio, coming to me distantly from the kitchen.

I remove my coat and boots, sling myself down on the sofa and put my feet up. I sit and I listen, hearing the soft murmur of the logs on the fire.

Sure enough, before long I'm aware of a car approaching down the lane. It stops. I hear the car-doors slam and muffled voices, followed by a loud knock that almost makes the house shake.

"Merry Christmas!"

It's Sarah, beaming at me as I open the front door, as usual waving a bottle in each hand.

"Happy Christmas," I laugh.

"This is Paul," Sarah says half turning to introduce her new partner who is now following her through the front door. A kiss for her and a shake of the hands for him. "Paul... Ed, Ed... Paul," she introduces us. "Oh fantastic, you've got a fire going, it's so nice and warm in here. It didn't start snowing till we got to Newstead. They said it would. How lovely for Christmas Eve... We're going to have a white Christmas for once..." Sarah is obviously a little nervous showing off her new man.

"Nice to meet you," Paul says, and I return the compliment;

"You too. Let me take your coats," and as I turn to carry coats upstairs, the lounge door opens and there's a squeal of delight as Belinda comes through to greet our guests.

From upstairs I can hear excited chatter and introductions being made, for by now Belinda and Sarah have met several times, but this is the first time either of us have met the new Paul. Paul is a bus driver in Elchester. Sarah quite literally bumped into him when she reversed her car into his bus at the Longwater Shopping Centre. The day after the bus company cleared him of all wrong-doing, he asked her out.

"Who's for drinks?" I ask on coming back down.

"Wine for me," says Sarah.

"Paul, would you like a glass of wine, or do you prefer a beer?"

"Beer please, mate."

I return from the kitchen. Two beers, a glass of

wine and an orange juice. "Cheers everyone!" I say and we all settle down.

"Not drinking, Belle?" Sarah looks bemused.

Belinda smiles and takes my hand as we sit together on the sofa. We neither of us say anything, and I'm sure I'm smiling too. Sarah looks at the two of us, takes it all in, opens her mouth, puts down her glass and is immediately coming across the room putting her arms around Belinda first and then me.

"Congratulations! Congratulations!" she says, her eyes starting to fill with tears. "When's it due? Oh my God! What fantastic news! I'm just so happy for both of you."

"We haven't told anyone yet..." replies Belinda.

"Except our parents," I interject.

"... but we think, *he*, or *she*, is due around the end of May."

And I feel Belinda's hand softly squeeze my own.

*

We are sitting round the table in the back room. Our meal is finished and the old tin containing the letters is on the table in front of us. Sarah has been telling Paul all about our adventures earlier in the year. She is the only person that Belinda and I ever told about our escapade in the tunnel, and how she really *did* come to break her ankle. Paul wants to know what it will be like to sleep in a haunted house tonight, and so I have to disappoint him because since finding the diamonds in the tunnel, there have been no more instances where objects have disappeared mysteriously. No more eerie footsteps. No more spooky apparitions. Even the garden gate leading down to the railway tracks has behaved itself, no longer opening of its own accord.

"However, what I will always wonder..." I confess, "is whether, or not, the ghost - if that's what it was - was a good ghost or a bad ghost? I just assume it was the ghost of Mrs Weston, the crossing-gate keeper, who was here in the 1950s."

"Well she did lead you to the diamonds. Maybe that's what she was trying to do all along," answers Sarah, "so perhaps she wasn't all that bad?"

"But remember, she did push me into that cupboard upstairs and somehow, I ended up in the railway tunnel," Belinda argues. "I don't call that very *good*!"

I agree: "Yes, and into the path of two oncoming trains!"

"Ghost trains?" asks Paul.

"I don't think so. They seemed real enough to us. I'm sure we were nearly killed."

"What did you do with the diamonds?" asks Paul again.

"I handed them in to the police; said I'd found them in the loft. Last I heard, the diamond dealers in Antwerp were very excited by it all."

"Weren't you tempted to keep them?"

"Not for long. I don't know anything about such things, never mind how to sell them. But I'm hoping I might get offered some sort of a reward when their rightful owner is traced." I ponder for a moment. "No, I think Robert Wallace had stolen those diamonds and Mrs Weston died in the tunnel, hit by a train, whilst trying to hide them in there or trying to retrieve them after he was hanged. These must be the letters that he sent her, arranging to meet, and she kept them hidden in the tin - until I found them again when I was putting things up into the attic. Perhaps the tunnel - or somewhere near it - was where they used to meet, so that she could avoid their affair being found out. Remember she would have had first-hand knowledge of when trains were due, and when the line would be free from traffic."

"Yes," adds Belinda, "I don't think she went in there to commit suicide, after her lover was executed, romantic as that might sound. After all, why go in there to do it?"

"Maybe she was pregnant with Robert Wallace's child," suggests Sarah creatively, "and after he got executed she knew her husband would find out, once there was a baby on the way."

The candles on the table quiver irritably and one of them goes out. There must be a draught coming from somewhere.

"So," Paul asks, "Mrs Weston was definitely your ghost?"

I pause again, still somewhat reluctant to believe that I had actually been haunted, despite all that had happened. Or maybe, even here amongst these three people, unwilling to own up to something that many would say was just a fanciful story. Whilst I try to decide, the remaining candlelight dances on our faces and the clock on the wall still ticks. I'm uncomfortable again with that tin of letters sitting there on the table looking at me. The house has seemed different since finding those diamonds in the tunnel - like a drifting vessel finally grounding upon some mainland shore. It has adapted to suit its new purpose; there are two of us living here now, and, of course, a third is on the way.

As I'm willing myself to answer Paul's question, there's a loud thump on the front door that makes us all jump. Sarah gasps and drops a piece of cutlery. Paul raises his eyebrows. Belinda puts her hand to her chest, saying, "Whoever can that be? It's gone nine o'clock!"

Everyone looks at me. "Someone caught out in the snow?" I suggest peevishly, shrugging my shoulders.

"Only one way to find out," says Sarah.

Still nobody is willing to move. Oh well, I suppose, it is *my* house, *my* front door.

As I reach the door, I hear the knock again louder this time, as if more impatient.

"Gwen!" I say, opening the door, to find Belinda's colleague there on the step, all tightly wrapped up in a large duffle coat, a woolly scarf, woolly gloves and a woolly hat. Hearing this brings Belinda through from the dining room. By this time Gwen is beating her arms on her thighs to stamp out the cold. She screws up her nose as if she's trying not to sneeze.

"I'm on my way to see your mother," she announces to Belinda, ignoring me. "I thought I might go with her to midnight mass. And I wanted to bring you this." She hands Belinda a small present.

"Come on in," says Belinda opening the gift. "You must be freezing out there on a night like this!"

She shakes her head. "It's not too bad if you keep up a brisk walk. And it has stopped snowing. I knew you'd still be up-and-about when I passed your previous guest on the way down the lane."

"Oh Gwen, these are lovely. But how... how did you know?" Belinda is holding a pair of tiny knitted booties that she's just unwrapped.

"I guessed," she replies rather smugly. "I have a sixth sense about these things. Just like when I first saw Ed. He might have been a bit wrapped up in himself, but I knew you and he were going to get together."

I'll say one thing for Gwen: she does have her mysterious ways.

Belinda gives Gwen a hug and a kiss.

"What did you mean about our previous guest?" I ask. "You said you met someone coming down the lane."

"A woman," says Gwen. "She never replied when I wished her a Merry Christmas. Only wearing a thin gauze dress; no coat. I watched her go straight past me, and she vanished into the hedgerow."

I step out of the open front door. The yew trees opposite glisten with snow as the moon peers out from behind the clouds. Silvery light flickers over the front of *Railway Cottage* like animated shadows on the back wall of a cave. Sure enough there are some footprints leading away from the house and up the lane, totally distinct from Gwen's which come in the other direction. Sarah is suddenly standing next to me, on my left. She realises what I'm looking at, having overheard the conversation, and gives my arm a nudge. Then Belinda is next to me too. We are - all three of us - on the doorstep gazing at the footprints leading away through the snow; away from the house and away from us. Perhaps this is the final sign.

Belinda takes my hand and places it carefully on her tummy.

"Ed," she whispers. "I just felt the baby move."

ABOUT THE AUTHOR

Robert Guthrie grew up in Norfolk but now lives in Kent. As he contemplated leaving the teaching profession, he wrote this, his first novel.

Printed in Great Britain
by Amazon